Let Sleeping Dogs Lie

By Tiffani Quarles-Sanders

Hollow Bridge Publishing

Montgomery, AL 36108

Copyright 2019 by Tiffani Quarles-Sanders

ISBN: 978-0-9863319-9-2

Editing by Erika's Editing

Contents

"He's gone, Ms. Nowden," Misty said gently as she removed her fingers from the side of David Cayson's neck. Misty had been David's primary nurse since the day he'd entered hospice almost two months ago. She hoped her being here in David's final moments offered Debra a small measure of comfort.

A sob rose up from Debra's throat, sharp and piercing, as if the cancer pains that had ravaged David's body were now her own. Her husband had fought as hard as he could right up until they'd had no choice but to seek palliative care. And he'd loved Debra without fault up until the moment that his body had failed him.

"Ms. Nowden, you just take your time," continued Misty as she placed a soft hand on Debra's shoulder. "Go ahead and stay with Mr. Cayson as long as you need to. Thirty-five years is a long time to be together, and there's no rush now." She leaned forward and clasped Debra's quivering hands between hers. "When you're ready, I'll call the funeral home of your choosing for you."

"Thank you." Debra sighed deeply as she wiped the hot tears from her face. "I appreciate all you've done. David specified the Paradise Funeral Home for his services." She managed a solemn half-smile to show her thanks.

Misty nodded at the grieving woman and returned the half-smile. "Let me move some of this stuff out of the way," she offered as she began detaching David's tubes, wires, and monitors. "Grown or not, your children don't need to see all this today."

Sadness stole the rest of Debra's words as she watched Misty remove the oxygen mask from her beloved's face. Her stomach reeled and rolled like it was folding itself into a navy knot. How many times, over the years, had David comforted her when her nerves surged like this?

"I'm here if you need me," Misty said as she began wheeling one of the monitors out of David's room. "Just use the call button."

"David," Debra whispered in a voice that she could barely hear herself. Tears streamed freely down her cheeks as she slid a light hand over his still-warm skin. Skin that she yearned to remember every freckle and wrinkle of. "Rest well, my love."

She sat for a long time, gazing at her husband's body. He was barely recognizable. In the last few weeks, he'd lost what little weight he'd still had left to lose, and then some. His skin, once glowing with vitality, had taken on a bluish tinge from a perpetual lack of oxygen. His hands remain twisted and knotted, as if they still remembered every second of his pain.

Debra was so lost in memorizing the creases along David's mouth that she didn't hear her children enter the room.

"Mom?" Chris asked, trying not to startle her.

"Yes, baby, he's gone." Debra choked out the words as best she could, acknowledging David's passing aloud for the first time.

Chris moved next to his mother, draped a steady arm across her shoulders, and pulled her into a hug. His sister Lauren, her face a solemn mask of sympathy, embraced the two of them at once.

Being brave for her children, Debra finally managed to whisper, "It's better this way," as she pulled away. "No more pain. But he always loved you like you were his own. Don't you ever forget that."

"No, Mom, we won't. We couldn't," said Lauren, pushing back her own tears. Chris nodded in agreement as his sister continued. "None of that makes any difference to us."

"Mom, if you're ready," began Chris, "we should start making some phone calls." He rubbed small, soothing circles across her back, hoping to give his aging mother strength.

"Maybe you could start doing that for me. Just let me sit here a while longer."

Chris nodded again, knowing that his mother needed time to be alone with her thoughts and the one true love of her life. Lauren stepped into the hall, motioning for her brother to follow.

Within an hour, David's closest friends began streaming in and out of the room. Each offered condolences to Debra, but she barely heard them—she'd lost herself in her own memories and preferred to stay there. Her children handled all the social niceties for her; Debra had no strength for false smiles or the false hope they implied. Only when she recognized an unmistakable voice spilling in from the doorway did she break out of her trance.

"You've been such a blessing, Misty, thank you for all you've done," James said before turning to enter the room that held David's lifeless body.

"I'm glad you came," Debra whispered somberly after James had greeted Chris and Lauren. "He'd want you here."

James' face contorted into something that wasn't quite a smile. "Of course. I don't think there's anyone else left among us who knew David longer than I did." With a heavy heart, he sat down next to Debra and turned his attention to his friend of over sixty years.

Even though he could no longer feel it, James was careful to use his lightest touch as he reached forward and clasped David's thinned shoulder. "David, we been through it all," he began. "You were my brother, the closest I had to a brother on this Earth." James, who usually had the voice of a gentle giant, choked out his words. He lifted his head toward the ceiling to keep his welling tears from falling onto his cheeks. "First Big Jim, and now you," he uttered before wracking sobs overcame him. Too much, too fast.

Lauren made her way across the room, placed her hands on James' shoulders, and began massaging away the tension in his neck. She didn't know what else to do.

"If it weren't for Big Jim building where he did, David and I never would've been friends, you know. His estate was so big it sprawled right on over to our side of town. My family and I, we lived just down the road from there." James paused before chuckling sadly. "An' David and I would get up to all sorts of antics—though my mama didn't much like me hanging out with a white boy."

"I know," replied Lauren sadly. "David told us all about it. Many times. He loved you like a brother, too."

At Lauren's words, a moan straight from the pit of James' soul escaped from his lips. Debra, Lauren, and Chris all surrounded him even more closely, trying to offer what little comfort there was to be had.

"Thank you again for callin' me," James finally said. He hesitated before continuing. The last thing he wanted was to broach this subject, but he also knew he was the only one who could. "But I need to ask, have you called Mary and her kids?"

Debra felt her blood pressure rise. Frustration slid in where sadness once sat. She gritted her teeth and shot a look at Chris, all but begging him to answer the question for her.

Chris jumped in, but his words failed him. "No, I… we… that is…"

"It's alright, I can call for you," offered James. "It won't take the family but an hour or two to get here, an' those kids deserve their closure, too."

"We are his family," Debra hissed, unable to control herself. She needed that point to be clear. "Those sons of his always blamed me for their parents breaking up. And Mary won't tell them the truth to save her soul, either. Her marriage to David was over way before he and I met."

"James is right, though, Mom," said Lauren. "They should know. They should have a chance to say their goodbyes before we call the Paradise."

"Are you taking her side?" snapped Debra.

"Of course not, Mom. But maybe it would—" Debra shot her daughter a glare so sharp that it made the rest of her Lauren's sentence disappear behind pursed lips.

"If they really wanted to see him, they should've come." Debra cut her hands across the air swiftly. "They knew David was… real bad. James told them as much not two days ago."

"I did, yes," squeaked James. The last thing he wanted was a fight with Debra, but he also didn't want to face Mary's considerable wrath. The two women had settled into a sort of truce-by-distance since Mary had moved to Selma ten years ago, but the vitriol between the two still burned white-hot. There was no good answer to this problem, and he knew it.

"That settles it then!" cried Debra as she shot up from her chair and pushed the call button. "I'm not arguing with you about this."

"Mom, James can make the call, you don't have to," Lauren said, trying, but not succeeding, at keeping her voice calm and even. "You don't even have to be here if they come. This is no time for compounding pain. I understand—"

Misty popped her head into the room, cutting Lauren off. "What can I do for you, Ms. Nowden?"

Debra shot one more seething glance at James, Chris, and Lauren before her eyes turned soft and sorrowful again. With a deep breath, she coughed out the words that would end a decades-long chapter in her life.

"We're ready." Debra exhaled. "Please call the Paradise."

Chapter 2

"Our appointment is at nine o'clock," Debra called

out. She tapped a beat against the knob of the front door with

her tattered fingernail. "We'll be late if we don't leave now."

"Coming," Chris yelled back. As her practical child,

her son only put as much effort into something as was

needed. In Debra's eyes, it was her son's one true flaw.

"Chris!" she cried again after another minute. "David

didn't like lollygagging." Debra was in no particular rush to

plan David's services, but her husband had always been a

stickler for time. She'd done everything in her power to keep

David happy in life, and she didn't want to disappoint him in

death.

Chris appeared at the top of the stairs, pulling on his

shirt as he walked. "I know, Mom. We're going to get there,

don't worry. Neither David nor the funeral home is going

anywhere. They can't do anything without you."

"I suppose that's true enough," Debra replied with a sigh as she urged her son through the door, "but David always said that tardiness stained his good name. There's no cause for that, not now. So get in the car and let's go."

At the dimly lit Paradise Funeral Home, a chill squirmed through Debra the instant she stepped through the door. Suddenly she was terrified of the fifteen feet between the entrance and the receptionist's desk. Once she'd crossed that threshold, she would officially be planning the funeral of the only man ever to love her to a fault. Her feet now felt like weights and her mouth like glue. She tried to will herself forward, but her legs would not move. Only when Chris pressed the palm of his hand gently into her back did Debra manage to step forward.

The receptionist, in her jarring, flamingo-pink dress, stepped out from behind her desk. "Good morning, how may I help you, ma'am?" she asked as she took the folder of paperwork from Debra's clenched hands.

She didn't reply until Chris urged her gently. "It's alright, Mom," he whispered.

Debra cleared her throat and swallowed the emotion threatening to escape. "I'm here to make arrangements for my husband, David Cayson," she explained. She shifted her clutch so that it fit even more tightly in the crook of her arm. "Our address and phone number are on the front of that folder."

"Oh yes, we should have him listed here." The receptionist slid her acrylic nail down a list of names. "Okay, Mrs. Cayson, let me—"

"—No!" Debra interrupted with a sharpness that surprised even herself.

The startled receptionist looked Debra up and down with as much confusion as Debra had pain.

"I'm not Mrs. Cayson, I'm Ms. Nowden," Debra corrected in a gentler voice. "David and I were together for decades, but we weren't legally married. We were man and wife in our own eyes, in our own hearts."

The receptionist nodded in understanding as she handed the folder back to Debra. "Please do pardon me. We are so sorry for your loss, Ms. Nowden." The smile returned to her face as her next words bubbled out. "Do take a seat. We'll take care of everything you need. Mr. Bush will be with you shortly."

Chris guided his mother to a nearby chair. As she sat down, Debra could feel weariness tiptoeing through her. She yawned without even trying to hide it.

"Did you sleep at all last night, Mom?" Chris asked. She remembered her family asking her that question when Chris was a baby. Back then, they'd told her to put a little cereal in his bottle and promised he would sleep until the sunrise. That worked surely enough, but now there was no easy fix for her sleep troubles.

"Some," she answered. Debra had managed three hours of sleep the night before. After hours of tossing and turning, she'd finally stopped fighting insomnia and decided to dig out as much of David's paperwork as she could find. She hated dealing with these types of details, and she hoped the Paradise could fill in any of the gaps she'd missed.

"Good morning, Ms. Nowden." The deep-voiced man slid into the foyer so smoothly that Debra never heard his footsteps. From his coal-colored eyes to his black suit, everything about the slender man was dark, except for his tie. It was flamingo pink, the exact same shade as the receptionist's dress.

"I'm Frank Bush, the funeral director." He extended his hand, "I'll be handling all of your needs. Thank you for choosing the Paradise Funeral Home. Step this way."

"I received some information about Mr. Cayson's life insurance yesterday," Mr. Bush began once they were seated in his office, "but it does seem to be incomplete."

"Yes, I sent some paperwork over after they picked up his remains yesterday. I didn't have all the policy information at the time, but this should help." Debra explained as she handed her folder to Mr. Bush. "He had a seventy-five-thousand-dollar policy That's more than enough to cover your finest services."

"Allow me a moment to review this, please." The still and straight man flipped through the paperwork without moving his torso once. Debra and Chris sat equally still in the awkward silence.

"I see... I do believe..." The words curled off Mr. Bush's lips as if he were unsure of what to say next. "The insurance itself looks fine, but there does seem to be an issue."

A knot formed in Debra's stomach once again. What possible problem could there be? David was a punctual man who paid all his bills on time. Debra ran the household finances from their linked account, but David had taken care of everything else. Profits, investments, savings, registrations, college funds, insurance, policies, deeds—she never had to give any of that a thought. That had always been their way.

"What's the problem?" Chris asked bluntly. His mother didn't need any additional strain and he resented Mr. Bush for pushing it onto her.

Mr. Bush looked up from the paperwork. "Who is Mary Cayson?"

His words may as well have been bullets. Between her lack of sleep and the sadness sitting in her, Debra very nearly yelled unladylike things at the man. Who was Mary Cayson? Mary Cayson was not the woman sitting in front of him. Mary Cayson was not the woman who'd spent the last thirty-five years at David's side, nor was she the woman who'd come to bury him.

Debra took a deep breath. She didn't say any of those things. "She's his first wife," she explained with all the civility she had in her. "They've been separated for close to forty years now. She stays in Selma."

"Mr. Cayson listed her listed as his beneficiary," Mr. Bush answered in a clipped tone as he lifted a document from the folder for Debra to see. "Are you the executor of his estate, perhaps? Or do you have his will?"

"No, I don't." Debra shook her head, partly to answer the question, but mostly to clear the mounting fear crowding her mind. She didn't understand what Mary had to do with any of this, not when she'd been by David's side day and night. When he'd first gotten sick, Debra was the one who bathed him, she was the one who administered his medicines, she was the one who'd placed heating pads on his aching chest and stroked this thinning hair with love.

"David handled most everything in that vein," Debra explained. Only when he got sick did I start doing more, but either he or his accountant still signed the checks."

Mr. Bush leaned forward and slid the folder across his desk back to her. "Do you have anything, anywhere that shows power of attorney? A notarized document, something?"

More knots tightened in Debra's stomach and connected to ones that had already formed. They lump they created were invading her chest as well. She could barely breathe. "No. Every month, David had his financial manager transfer funds to my account, and I kept our household running from that. If I wanted anything more, David took care of it before I even had to ask."

Mr. Bush leaned his narrow body back in his chair and steepled his fingers. "Help me to understand, so that I can help you." He paused, putting together his next words carefully. "Mr. Cayson divorced his first wife, and the two of you have been living in common-law marriage together since?"

"Yes, that's right." Debra nodded her head furiously. She needed this man to understand that she was sincere, that David was her world. "Except that he never fully divorced Mary. For legal reasons."

Frank Bush didn't reply. Instead, he buried himself back into the paperwork, flipping through the pages once again. Quiet blanketed the room. Debra knew that she was still alive because she could hear her heart thumping as it raced in her chest.

Panic swept through her. A wife saw her husband through until the last shovelful of dirt dropped onto the casket. She couldn't walk away from this day, from her life with David, without completing her job.

"And what about your children?" Mr. Bush asked suddenly. "Any biological children together?"

"My sister and I, we never wanted for anything, never even came close to it." Chris interjected. "David treated us as his own, but no, technically we're not kin. And we were really too old for adoption when he and my mother came together."

"I see. In that case, Ms. Nowden—"

"—Mr. Bush," Debra cut in before pausing to inhale and exhale. She needed to control the quiver slipping into her voice. "I need to make arrangements for my husband. He told me when we laid his father to rest that he wanted his services handled by the Paradise, so that's what I'm going to do."

Mr. Bush shook his head as if he didn't have a voice for his words, yet there was sympathy stirring in his dark eyes. Debra could tell that on any other day, he was probably a very nice man, but on this day, in this office, Frank Bush was her enemy.

Mr. Bush's voice took on a still, formal quality. "At the Paradise Funeral Home, we only make arrangements with the next of kin unless other mechanisms have been put in place. That's been our policy since my grandfather's time. We will only speak with his legal wife, Mary Cayson."

Debra blinked. She'd heard his words, and even saw this man's mouth move, but none of it made any sense. She opened her mouth to speak, but nothing came out.

Mr. Bush stood up from his desk and began walking toward the door. "And only Mary Cayson is entitled to Mr. Cayson's life insurance." He opened the door widely, effectively ending their meeting. "I'm sorry, Ms. Nowden, but unless I have permission from Mary Cayson, I cannot give you any additional information."

Chapter 3

"Who were you talking to?" Brenda asked before James could even end the call on his cell phone.

James turned to his wife, who was looking at him over the top her glasses, which she needed for reading her sheet music. He could often tell how upset Brenda was by how low her glasses were on her nose. Right now, his wife's glasses told James that she was merely curious. "I was talking to Debra," he answered dutifully. He'd learned long ago that the best way to stay on the route to happiness with Brenda was to tell her everything, every day, as soon as he knew it. Her mind was too sharp and her curiosity too wide for anything less.

Brenda leaned forward and closed her songbook. She'd been playing slowly and dolefully this evening. James had been watching the nightly news with the sound muted and the captions turned on. More and more, this had become their after-dinner ritual, especially now that they were both retired.

"Debra?" she questioned. "How is she? Does she need anything?" Debra and Brenda had had their dust-ups over the years, but Brenda wouldn't turn her back on a woman in mourning.

"Seems she's in a tight spot," replied James, "and I don't know if I can help. To start with, apparently she needs Mary's approval to make the arrangements for David. The Paradise won't have it any other way."

"That's insulting! On what grounds!" The words shot out of Brenda's mouth as she closed the fallboard harder than she intended. A loud, atonal thwack resonated across the room.

James slid his cell phone across the top of the upright piano and shook his head. "Well, you know Mary's still his legal wife. They never did get a divorce."

"What?! I didn't know anything about that," exclaimed Brenda as her eyebrows nearly shot up past her hairline, which momentarily smoothed out the wrinkles around her eyes. When they'd first met fifty-something years ago, James had fallen all over himself at the site of Brenda's honey-colored eyes and full mouth. Over time, though, the sharp looks from her eyes and unrestrained words from her mouth sometimes pushed him away.

"That's why he never married Debra after all those years?" Brenda cried.

"Yep." There was no need to get into the rest of the details; he knew his wife's mind had already filled in the financial implications of a divorce. "An' since just about every dollar is in David's name, Debra needs the life insurance policy to bury him. But Mary's the beneficiary of that, too."

Brenda stood up and stuffed her songbook into the piano bench, then slid her reading glasses down her nose.

"That's a bunch mess. That's why I tell everybody, what's done in darkness will come to light."

James turned off the television. The news would have to wait. "No darkness here. David loved Debra so much that she was the only one after Mary. Love is light. Ain't that what you always tell me?"

"What about the house? The cars? The investments?" Brenda swatted her hand through the air with the mention of each asset.

"All in David's name. He didn't even leave a will, at least not that we know of."

"See," Brenda started, more shocked than ever, "God doesn't like ugly. Love might be light, but that doesn't mean it can be stupid. Debra never should've allowed that, and David should've put his affair in order. It's not like the man didn't know he was dying."

"Brenda!" James shouted. "We don't speak ill of the dead in this house!" The wound on his heart was still too fresh for criticisms. "The good Lord forgives, and so should we."

"You know I'm right." She waggled her head with each word. "I never would've put myself in that kind of situation. There never would've been a future with me if David hadn't gotten his past right. I would've told Debra as much, too, if I'd known."

"Debra ain't you. David didn't love you," James declared. For all her brains, Brenda never always had trouble holding her tongue. James accepted that for the most part, but right now he needed peace. Normally he was a patient man, but now he needed peace enough to mourn.

"Now look what's happened! And maybe Debra deserves it, too. She and David were waiting all those years for Big Jim to go to glory just to inherit Cayson Construction. But Big Jim's estate isn't even settled yet, and David didn't last four more months before he was walking on the other side, too. That's the work of the Almighty himself."

"You not gon' sit here and speak on my friend like that," James growled. "An' it's not up to you to divine what God does-and-does-not do. You should know as well as I do that David and Debra took good care of Big Jim. David loved that man."

"That's not exactly how I saw it. Big Jim wasn't his real father anyway. He didn't care for David enough to put legal paperwork behind it, either."

"That's not how it was! Martha and Big Jim took David in after her sister died. You weren't there, you didn't see it with your own eyes! And I *know* you're not tellin' me adopted parents can't love their children like their own!"

Brenda took a breath, eased up some. In their long years together, she'd never seen anyone claim a child as fiercely as her husband had claimed Tonya. James had loved her with tenderness and acceptance from the moment she was born; woe to anyone who tried to tell him that he wasn't daddy to her little girl.

"Of course not, I'm not saying that at all," she began more gently. "But our family doesn't have wealth like that to poison the well water. All that money that David was plotting to get, and Debra was plotting to spend. Now neither of them will see any of it. They're having bad luck because they had bad intentions."

"Do I need to remind you what those two did for this family?" James shot as anger roiled up through his very core. "David hired me as a foreman at a time when black men *couldn't be* foremen! And he kept me by his side ever since! Forty-five years of paychecks from Cayson Construction is the reason we get to retire in ease. They're the reason we got that nice piano for you to play. And who put Tonya through college, huh? David's money, but that was Debra's doing. All that was bad intentions?"

"You can stop trying to defend them," Brenda shot back, angry again. "Everybody but you knew David and

Debra had enough ugly ways underneath it all to break a mirror."

"Stuff from the streets don't belong in this house!" James shouted. "They did good by us! So stop your speculating."

"Mama, what y'all in here arguing about?" Tonya called as she walked through the door. "I can hear you two all the way outside. This ain't like you at all. What's happened?"

James relaxed at the sound of his daughter's voice. No matter what the situation, his baby girl always made him feel better, and she was the balm he needed right now.

Brenda rolled her eyes at her husband before hugging their daughter. "Nothing, baby—we've just had some news, is all. About David's estate. Ev-e-ry-thing is going to Mary."

"Whaaatt!" Tonya gasped. "There must be some mistake. David would never do that to his own wife."

Brenda filled her daughter in on the details. Tonya's eyes grew wide in shock as she listened.

"Debra will be homeless before David is in the ground if Mary has anything to do with it," Tonya finally said. "Daddy, can't you do anything?"

"I don't know, baby, I'll try," James answered softly. "I'll think on it some."

"I can't believe any of this. I just saw Debra last week. Our literacy program at the community center is really taking off. No matter what was going on with David, she still volunteered as much as she could. Twice a week, at least."

"We all do what we can for each other," James encouraged, a tenderness in his tone. "Even when we're in need, we can still help others."

"But now everything's different, upside-down. I hate it when things change all sudden like this." Tonya stomped her foot in frustration, as if she'd suddenly morphed from a fifty-year-old woman into a little girl. She looked up at her father pleading eyes. "It's not right, Daddy."

James never could take seeing his daughter even the slightest bit upset. He reached out and put his arm around her. "I know, this is hard on everyone, honey. But the world's gon' keep on changin' whether we like it or not." He hugged her even more tightly as purposefully changed the subject. "Enough about that, now. What are you doing here? We weren't expecting you tonight."

"I just came to pick up my extra cell phone charger. I left it here last weekend, and I just now had time to swing by. Mark and I are down to one car, and he's running a workshop tonight at the church. They needed a CPA—it's a program for first-time homebuyers."

James's eyebrows wrinkled with concern. "You know you can always use my car if you need it." He patted his daughter's shoulder. "Your mother and I don't do a lot."

"Thank you, Daddy, but Mark and I have a tip on a good used car." Tonya took her father's hand in hers. "A new one would be better, but we'd rather buy what we can afford outright and avoid financing. It's the smarter move with both Alaysa and Jamal in college."

Before he could help himself, James shot a look at his wife. "See? David and Debra freed us of that burden, freed our daughter from years of paying off college loans."

Brenda rolled her eyes hard in response. She turned to her daughter and asked, "Are you coming to David's services?"

"I'm afraid not Mama. I have my recertification classes next week. That's not something I can miss—not even on account of a family friend. I'd like to be there for Debra, but…"

"Your career is important, baby." Brenda agreed. "Never you mind."

"And after hearing about this mess, truthfully I don't know if I should go anyhow. Daddy's the one person who's on good terms with both of them, and I don't want to be seen taking sides on that account."

"It would mean a lot to Debra if you could come, even if for a little while." James pleaded. It would mean a lot to him too. He needed some of her sweetness near him during such a sour time.

"Debra's been in my prayers, Daddy, but I'm sure there'll be some drama. I'm not trying to be a witness."

Brenda chuckled before she could help it. James sighed. Tonya did have a point, though. Her recertification classes were important, plus a part of him didn't want his daughter to see the ugliness he suspected was ahead.

"We sent Debra flowers today, and I'll donate a nice arrangement for the services, Daddy. And I'll check up on her too—she's always been good to me. But right now, I've got to go, or Mark will be late."

Brenda agreed and hugged her daughter goodbye. James walked his Tonya out. He didn't even hear the side door shut before Brenda picked up where they'd left off.

"I'm afraid this isn't going to turn out too well for Debra," she sighed, keeping her voice intentionally calm.

James shook his head. "Let it rest, honey. You and me, we're strong together. All *our* finances are in order, thanks to David. Let's just be grateful for that."

"James, I know this is… hard for you, but I just can't make any sense of this. Yes, they were generous enough to some—I'll concede that much—but greedy in their own way."

Before Brenda could say another word, James sliced a hand through the air, which told his wife that he had reached his limit: the subject was closed for the moment. "Look, we're not gon' talk about this anymore tonight. I'll go visit Mary tomorrow an' see if we can work this out."

"Work what out? Mary's been angry for so long, I don't think she knows how not to hate. Anger like that burns long and slow, but hotter than the fires of hell."

"At least I can try. If there's a way to be found here, it's my duty to David to lay down the path."

Brenda's expression softened. "I married you on your kindness, and I know you mean well, but listen to me." She looked James directly in the pupils as she said her next words. "When white folks get mad at each other, you need to stay out of it. This isn't your cross to bear."

Chapter 4

James had a good while to think about how he could

approach Mary and still keep all of his limbs. The drive from

Montgomery to Selma was just about an hour, and he knew

the road well. As he drove, his mind raced through the

various possibilities of how this meeting would go. He

played out various scenarios in his mind; none ended

especially well for him, but his sense of duty to David kept

him driving west along route eighty.

"Thank you, God, for allowing me to arrive safe in

Selma," James said aloud as he crossed the city line. He was

truly grateful. As a young man, when he'd bought his own

TV set, Bloody Sunday was the very first news story he'd

seen on that tiny, flickering screen. The images stayed with

him to this day.

Stretching Boston Ferns covered the wrap-around

porch of Mary's home. James pulled into the long driveway

with ease, then released a deep breath. He would do this for his friend. He would clean up this battlefield in David's honor. Hopefully.

He knocked gently on the door. He didn't want to alarm Mary, who always startled easily despite the fierceness she could unleash. He imagined that her sons, Jason and Meyer, would be at the house, too, but he wasn't sure. Both lived in Columbus, just over the state line into Georgia, and neither visited often. Over the years, their parents' strained relationship had eroded the family's bonds.

"James, is that you?" Mary squinted her aged eyes as she opened the door. "What are you doing here?" She squinted a moment longer as she opened the screen door, then finally smiled a bit with recognition.

"I came to check on you," James replied. It was partially true. He hoped the rest of the conversation would flow as easy as their greeting.

"Much appreciated. But you didn't have to drive all this way," Mary answered politely. If she knew James had another agenda, she didn't let on. She opened the door wider and ushered him into the atrium of her spacious home.

"Thank you. It's good to see you, despite the… circumstance."

Purposefully ignoring James' remark, Mary sniffed as she turned quickly and began leading him down the spotless corridor and into her sitting room. Mary always kept her home immaculately clean. Anyone who dared to could put on a white glove, slide a finger along the baseboards or furniture, and still head to Sunday service with a perfectly sterile, unmarked glove. That same formality oozed from every part of Mary's aged, yet still stern and upright, frame.

"How's Tonya?" Mary asked pleasantly as they walked down the long hall.

James couldn't help but smile at the mention of his baby girl. He was so proud of all she'd accomplished. "She got herself promoted last year to head nurse on her ward, and she's a full nurse practitioner now," he replied. "And otherwise doing well, thank you."

As they entered the sitting room, a yapping Shih Tzu dog scampered across the polished hardwood floors then nipped at James' ankle, which was the last thing he needed right now. There was too much sadness in his heart, too much on his mind, too much nervousness in his gut.

"Have a seat. Can I get you something?" Mary asked before she sat down in her wingback recliner.

"No, thank you. Don't trouble yourself at all." He lowered himself onto the plush loveseat. The unyielding dog stayed at his ankle like he had hotdogs hidden in his hem. With his foot, he firmly but carefully pushed the Shih Tzu away. Fortunately, the little dog took the hint and trotted across to Mary, where it sat itself expectantly at her feet.

James' mind was working a mile a minute with dread, but he knew the situation was delicate enough to warrant a good deal of social niceties before bringing up the reason for his visit. And he wasn't without compassion for Mary. She could be a hard woman, but that didn't change her right to grieve.

"I wanted to offer my condolences in person," James began, keeping his voice tempered and even. "How are the kids holding up?"

The change in Mary's composure was striking and swift. Her stiff, straight shoulders slumped; her face followed their lead. Her softened gaze landed on the floor, and she sighed with a vulnerability that James had never heard in her before. He considered canceling his mission. Maybe it was too soon.

At that moment, James remembered the years when both Mary and David had perpetually worn that similar sour looks on their faces. It wasn't until David finally left the house for good that either of them reflected any peace in their eyes.

Then, as sure as she had slid into soft, Mary's face jumped straight into the consternation that so often crossed her features. "They're doing well enough, I guess," she answered. "They're driving in this evening. They'll be here soon."

"The company will do you good, I expect."

"Do you know that woman of David's didn't even call us so we could say our goodbyes?" she suddenly hissed. James was relieved that she'd brought up Debra, but the tone she used was scathing. He decided it was best not to mention his own private goodbye to David.

Mary shook her head before continuing with an even greater severity. "Mark my words, she's going to pay for the evil she's done. She didn't just take my husband, she turned my own children against me. And now I'm an old woman living alone, when I should have my sons by my side. I've got grandkids that hardly know me from Eve. All because of that hussy!"

"I'm so sorry, Mary. I have no doubt that David loved your boys and cared for you, too." He didn't want to add any more fuel to the fire, at least not yet, and so he let his words hang in the air.

After a moment, and now with a wistfulness in her tone, Mary said, "David and I were so young when we first met… it almost seems like another life."

"It's true," answered James, "we're all generous with age these days." He added a soft smile, hoping to ease Mary up even more.

The two spent the next half-hour reminiscing. Mary wanted to talk about her first year with David, just after they were married and were living in a cottage on Big Jim's estate. James couldn't deny her that much, but as he listened, he couldn't help but feel that Mary's happy memories were crowding out the bad ones. And having been by David's side when the two had separated, James knew there were more than enough bad memories to go around.

As easy as a social visit would be, James knew he had to say his piece. If he didn't, the guilt would peck at him for years, he was sure of that much. There had to be a way to resolve all this, something he'd been missing.

"Mary," he began, trying not to let his voice tremble as his nerves rose. "Forgive me if this isn't the time, but I'd like to help you with David's estate. David and I were near-like family, and I do want to make sure everything is taken care of the right way."

"That's kind of you, but I have all that covered," answered Mary. "I called Mr. McLemore this morning. I was, and I still am, David's wife—all his assets go to me. And, providing there are no hiccups, David's inheritance of Big Jim's holdings will come to me, too." The Shih Tzu yipped sharply and wagged its tail as if it were celebrating Mary's new wealth.

"Well, that is a blessing. David did look after you. With or without Big Jim's estate, you and your boys will have more than enough to live comfortable." James forced a sad smile onto his face before lowering his voice. "But Mary, I'm here to ask that *everyone* in David's life be provided for."

Mary's eyes instantly turned into knives. "I know you're not here begging for that Jezebel!" she snapped viciously. "She had David all those years. This is my time now!"

Recoiling at Mary's fierceness, James looked down at the floor and began picking at his thumbnail. He didn't know what to say to that, but he knew he needed to press on.

"I understand, but what you have to consider *is*. You and your kids are about to become millionaires several times over, while Debra's name ain't even on her own home."

"I know it," spat Mary as leaped with surprising agility from her chair. "That woman never said one kind word to my boys about me. When they moved away all those years ago, I told that tramp I'd never forget. And I haven't.

My memory is long, and my money will soon be even longer."

James winced but quickly collected himself. "Mary, please. She's too old to start over now. Let her have at least the house. David would've wanted it that way."

Mary leaned forward and slammed her flat palm on the coffee table, but she kept her voice eerily steady and low. "You knew my husband. If he wanted that woman to be taken care of, he would've made provisions. Let her move in with that lazy son of hers. It's no concern of mine."

James tried again. "Thirty-five years. Surely she deserves someth—"

"—There are *rules* to this life, and she broke one too many! There's a judgment day for us all." Mary's gaze never faltered as her words sliced across the room.

He nodded his head and sighed heavily. There was no use in arguing, her mind had been fixed before James had walked up to the door. He'd have to find peace in knowing he'd tried to do the right thing.

"James, you were good to my husband, and to my boys when they were first coming up. But I do very much suggest," and here Mary paused as she pointed a knotted finger at him, "that you keep any ideas on this subject to yourself!"

James opened his mouth to reply but immediately closed it again. Mary kept her cold gaze trained on him a moment longer, and then, without another word, bent down and scooped up her barking Shih Tzu. By the time she met his eyes again, she had slipped on her polite-and-proper mask. A mask that was somehow just as terrifying as her anger.

"Now you'll have to excuse me," Mary said with enough saccharine sweetness to give anyone a stomachache, "because I do need to prepare. My boys will be here soon.

You know this house well enough, you may show yourself

out."

Chapter 5

"Mom, are you sure you want to do this?" Chris asked hesitantly. "Maybe you… shouldn't go where you aren't wanted. Maybe we should… sit down with Mary at another time, when everyone is less emotional."

"I can't believe the nerve of that bitch—trying to stop me from going to my own husband's funeral!"

Two days ago, Debra had received a certified letter stating that she wouldn't be welcome at David's services. Mary had hired a security team, which would escort Debra out of the church if she attended. A threat which didn't deter her in the slightest.

"We could have our own memorial and invite our friends," Chris suggested as he unclicked his seatbelt. "We could honor David and still keep what little peace there is."

Debra's entire body recoiled in shock as she clutched at her chest. She shot her son an accusatory look, as if his suggestion were betrayal itself. "That's not the same, and you know it. I need to see David one last time. And I don't understand why you can't get behind me on this. You're my son!"

"Mom, you know I'm here for you," he reminded his mother meekly. "But this is about… look, Mom, Lauren is already inside. Our family is represented. You should leave it there."

"We're going to this funeral! I birthed you. I gave you life. You're doing this for me!" The fury that flashed across her face morphed into hot, angry tears. Two or three heavy drops fell from her eyes before she could stop them. "No one has the right to stop me from seeing my husband laid to rest!" she roared as she pounded the dashboard with her fist. "I will honor him!"

Chris reached over and took his mother's hand, just like he had as a little boy. He hoped the familiar touch would calm her, even though the angry, grieving woman sitting next to him now didn't seem at all like the mother he knew. The two sat there together in silence for a moment with only the whirring of the car's engine surrounding them.

"Mom, you can't honor David if you and Mary are fighting in front of the casket," he said somberly but gently. "You can't honor him if everyone is focused on you."

"That shitty piece of paper won't stop me!" Determination pushed Debra's eyebrows so close together that they touched. To Chris' dismay, she stepped out of the car, then slammed the door shut as if Mary's face were the hinge.

Chris cut the ignition as he scrambled after his mother. Debra stood ten feet away, staring up at the church and planning the best route across the grassy parking lot. People mulled in small groups by the church's stairs, but she didn't see any security.

Mary, in her vanity, had chosen the largest church in Montgomery for the services. If Debra had had her way,

David would've been laid to rest much more modestly—a respectful service at their home congregation, without any garishness. One more insult to this day.

Grass and soft earth squished beneath the high heels that Debra had worn on her last night out with David over two years ago—he'd always liked her in heels. They clicked loudly against the concrete steps once Debra reached the church. Chris followed five steps behind his mother, hoping the scene he knew was coming wouldn't be too much.

Even before she'd taken even a full step into the large vestibule, Mr. Bush appeared. "Ms. Nowden, you need to stop." He held his hand in the air as if the force of his five fingers would magically halt her. She ignored the slender man as if he'd never spoken.

The funeral director jogged to get ahead of Debra's long determined strides as he barked into his walkie-talkie. Almost instantly, coming in from the side doors, four burly men formed a wall in Debra's path.

"You need to stop," Mr. Bush repeated. "I'm sorry for your loss, but the widow and grieving family have explicitly requested that you be denied entry."

"You won't keep me from him!" Debra cried as she attempted to push past the line of men. In response, two guards grabbed her by the arms. "You don't scare me, you brutes!" she yelled, trying to squirm out of the grip.

"Mom, please!" begged Chris. "David wouldn't want a scene! He had no taste for ugliness."

"He was my husband. Mine. He loved me!" Debra managed to push a step or two closer to the sanctuary where David lay. "I need my husband!"

"Go home, Ms. Nowden. This is no place for a scene," pleaded Mr. Bush.

The door to the sanctuary swung open as an usher, alarmed at the commotion, stepped into the doorway. Debra craned her neck, trying to get one last look at her husband.

The distraction was all the guards needed. One of them grabbed her by the waist and lifted her an inch from the floor.

"Chris, go in there and be with your sister!" Debra commanded as she fought against all three guards. "Tell her to stay put! David was your family, too."

Unsure of what to do, Chris looked around the vestibule in confusion before meeting Mr. Bush's eyes. Frank Bush nodded his head. "Mrs. Cayson made no other stipulations on entry. You may go in, if you wish."

Not able to watch the scene, Chris scurried into the sanctuary without another word. Mr. Bush turned to the usher. "Please instruct our guests to use the east door for the time being. I'll signal to you when this situation… resolves."

The guard restraining Debra from behind moaned as she landed an elbow in his gut. She was glad of his pain. She would kick, scream, and cry if it got her to David.

"Ms. Nowden, we need you to leave before we call the sheriff," Mr. Bush stated emphatically. "There are many people mourning today. You are disturbing them."

"And none of those people were David's wife for the last thirty-five years! I lived for David. I watched him die. Let me go!"

Before the somber funeral director could respond, James stepped out of the sanctuary. His eyes widened in shock as he panned the scene. Debra, still in the security guards' grip, no longer looked like the dignified woman he knew her to be. Her lipstick was now smeared across her face, and one high heel had flown off her foot. Her clutch, with its contents spilled, lay on the floor.

"Let her go now!" James demanded as he turned to Mr. Bush. "Is this how the Paradise Funeral Home treats its guests?"

"She is not a guest of the Paradise, or of the grieving widow," Frank Bush answered abruptly. "Unfortunately, Ms. Nowden is... having trouble accepting that."

"James!" Debra shouted, bowing her back against the guard. "You were David's best friend. Tell them! Tell him I'm his real wife!"

"Debra, I love you and David like family, but this isn't the place." James pleaded. "If you leave right now, I'll make sure we work everything out with Mary. You jus' can't be a part of this service." He moved closer to her. She was still crying, but not jerking and kicking quite as much.

"I should be in there," Debra shouted, but with much less force. "I should be with him." Her voice cracked as the tears streamed down her face.

"Gentlemen, give me some room," James instructed firmly as he opened his arms and embraced Debra and her sorrow. "Hush now, we'll work all this out later," he began gently, "but you have to understand, that this is what we have to do for today." He smoothed Debra's matted hair as she cried in his arms.

"Don't try to explain anything to her." Mary's shrill voice suddenly sliced through any peace that James had won. She pushed past Mr. Bush in a frenzy. "She wasn't anything to him. She was just his mistress, a plaything."

"How dare you speak to me that way!" The guttural yell that Debra unleashed erupted straight from the bottom of her soul. She broke free from James' arms and lunged at the one woman keeping her from her husband. Her eyes practically flashed red in anger.

A muscled arm locked around Debra again, but not before she'd made it only two feet from Mary. "David *left* you for a reason, you cold bitch!"

"You'd be sitting in that church if he really loved you! You'd have his last name! Mary hissed. "He would've let me go completely, but he didn't. You only wanted David's assets, and now you won't get a single penny."

"I never cared about his money! I loved David for David!"

"Ladies, please," cried James. "Let's find a way through this together. On another day."

Ignoring James, Mary leaned forward and in a loud, chilling, hiss, spat "It's a good thing you didn't love his money, then. You have one month to get out of my house. Exactly thirty days from today, or I'll have you arrested."

"I'm not leaving my home without a fight!" Debra yelled. She buckled against the security guard so hard that he nearly lost his grip.

"Perhaps if you'd been kinder to my boys, I might be more generous," Mary said with a false sweetness. "But you drove them from me with your evil ways."

In reply, Debra locked her burning eyes on Mary's, then spat on the floor.

Turning to the security guards, Mary commanded, "Get her out of here."

The two other guards grabbed Debra's arms, and all three men began pushing her toward the exit even as she continued to twist and turn and kick. The fourth guard scooped up Debra's purse and her one high heel and tossed them out onto the church steps.

Just as they were about to shove her through the doorway, Debra suddenly laughed manically. A vindictive echo filled the vestibule. "This isn't over, you bitch. I know the Cayson family secrets. David told me everything. Just you wait."

Chapter 6

David's voice echoed in Debra's head: "Sometimes you have to apply a little pressure to get the results that you deserve." Since David had left her with nothing else, Debra was going to use his advice to get what she *deserved* as his wife. Never once in all their years together—not even when he got sick—did Debra think her meticulous husband didn't have his final effects in order. But then again, David always had a terror of death. Years ago, when their accountant had suggested estate planning, David turned white as a ghost and then took to his bed for the evening. When his health took its first real turn for the worst, there'd been many a night when he'd cried out in his sleep, tortured by nightmares of death. She couldn't blame her husband for leaving this world without a will, although Debra knew no one else on Earth would understand that like she could. In her heart, she knew David trusted her to get her due.

Which was exactly what she was doing now as she stepped up to the reception desk at McLemore & Tinsley. She'd made a conscious decision to walk in with a smile on her face, even though the firm had neglected to reach out to her. McLemore & Tinsley had handled Cayson Construction's affairs for decades; David had been a VIP client, but apparently they'd now all but turned their back on her, much like so many others in her life had.

"Oh, Debra, good to see you. How are you holding up?" Tammy said as she stood up from her desk reached out for a hug. Tammy had been with the McLemore & Tinsley for over fifteen years, and her heart was as big as the law office was profitable. Even though the firm hadn't so much as sent Debra flowers, Tammy and her husband had sent her a card.

"These moments are always difficult," Debra answered as she pulled out of the hug. What else was she supposed to say?

"Yes. I'm so sorry, hun. Is there anything I can do for you?"

"I do need to see Stephen or Dennis," Debra answered. There was no use in dancing around what she'd come for. "There's a matter they need to be made aware of. Regarding Big Jim and my husband."

"Of course, of course," Tammy replied, although Debra noticed that the receptionist bristled ever so slightly at the word *husband*. It had been barely one week since David's funeral, and Debra knew what the waggling tongues of Montgomery were now telling their daughters: "Never stay with a man who doesn't marry you, or else you'll turn out crazy and broke like Debra Nowden."

"Well, Mr. Tinsley isn't here, but let me get Mr. McLemore for you. I'm sure he's   available," Tammy continued as she picked up the phone on her desk.

"Thank you." Debra thought about the secrets she was about to unleash upon McLemore & Tinsley. This was a big risk, but she had no other choice. Not if she was going to save her home. Not if she was going to claim what was rightfully hers.

Tammy gently placed the phone down back in the cradle. "Mr. McLemore said that he has an appointment in ten minutes. He'll call you with a time when he can schedule you in."

"Excuse me?" Debra had to double check to make sure she'd heard Tammy's words correctly. "Stephen doesn't have time? For me?" She'd never once been turned away from the firm, no matter how many times she and David had dropped in. Once, in an emergency, when McLemore & Tinsley was helping Debra get custody of Lauren and Chris, Stephen even left his own mother's birthday party to speak with them.

"That's what he said, hun, I'm sorry. You'll have to schedule an appointment," Tammy's smile faded as she spoke; like at all firms, clients fell in and out of favor all the time, but she hated this part of her job.

"Let's schedule for right now," Debra took advantage of Tammy's resignation, briskly moved past her desk, and barreled down the hall to Steven's office. Tammy, shocked, followed on Debra's heels.

"Stephen!" Debra glided through the office door as though she had been invited. "I need to talk to you. Right now."

"What are you doing back here?" he asked, clearly taken aback at Debra's insistence. "Tammy, I told you I had another appointment shortly."

"Yes, sir." Tammy nodded apologetically from behind Debra, "I tried to tell her as much, but she wouldn't listen." Her boss shot her an aggravated look, and Tammy retreated from the office.

"I'll say my piece," Debra proclaimed once Tammy was out of earshot. "A warning. Cayson Construction wouldn't want this to get out," she said, narrowing her eyes, "and neither would McLemore & Tinsley."

"I don't know what you're talking about, *Ms. Nowden*, but I'll give you three minutes." Stephen leaned all of his two-hundred-and-ninety-five pounds back in his sturdy swivel chair. "Say what you need to say, then leave."

"The way I see it, y'all have a problem," Debra began, dangling the information. She needed Stephen's full attention.

"What problem is that?"

"An image problem, to begin with, especially since you've neglected your due diligence. Maybe a legal problem, too, if the law finds McLemore & Tinsley guilty of suppressing evidence."

Stephen's expression shifted from angry to alarmed. He'd known Debra long enough to know she didn't make empty threats. He also knew that he and his longtime law partner weren't averse to stretching the definition of the word *legal* for their biggest clients.

Debra had planned out her words carefully. "It is just a shame really," she began smoothly. "You'd think this firm would give everyone their due. Plus, Cayson Construction takes so much pride in working with black and minority-owned companies, but—"

"—That's always been a point of pride for us and many of our clients," Stephen interrupted, trying to save face. He didn't like where this was going, and his mind had already flown to his retirement, which was planned for next year. The last thing he needed was a scandal.

"Then I'm sure you'll be shocked to know that Cayson Construction was responsible for the death of Montgomery's first independent black contractor." Debra all but crooned her words.

"You sound ridiculous." he snorted. "We've always had a strong relationship with the black community."

"How much are you willing to bet on the strength of that relationship?" She eyed the obese man in front of her. "Everyone loves a juicy story, and I'm sure you can see how this could cause you some problems. There are layers to this thing you can't begin to imagine."

"Hearsay! All hearsay. Where's your evidence?" he demanded. "McLemore & Tinsley will not be blackmailed!"

"There's plenty of evidence, Stephen. All you need to do is drive out to Lowndes County and ask about Willie Taylor."

Stephen sat forward and folded his arms across his desk. "I know nothing of a Willie Taylor at Cayson. There's a *James* Taylor, the foreman that retired a few years ago, but—"

"—Yes, he's Willie's first cousin on his mother's side."

"—*Willie* Taylor I've never heard of."

"No, you wouldn't have—although I'm sure he's in Cayson's files. He's been dead now for fifty years. He was part of the Cayson family—literally—and he was killed by Cayson Construction. In fact, a case could be made that Big Jim murdered…" Debra let her words hang in the air before she topped it with the real jewel, "…his own son. *With* David's blessing."

Stephen and his enormous belly shot up from his chair. He walked quickly around his desk, never once breaking eye contact with Debra. Finally, he announced "Big Jim had no biological issue, that's a well-known fact. A fact your late *partner* benefitted well from." Stephen said the word *partner* as if he were throwing a dagger straight at Debra's dignity.

"My *husband*," Debra shot back, told me everything after Big Jim died. "Willie was Big Jim's outside child, I've seen his birth certificate myself. You don't honestly think

Big Jim was faithful to Martha? With wealth like that, I bet he had Willie's mother for a song!"

"There's no need to be vulgar!" snapped Stephen. He ran his hand through what little hair was left on his head, gathering his thoughts. Then he walked back around his desk, pressed the intercom, and asked Tammy to cancel his meeting. With old dirt being unearthed, new business would have to wait.

"If this were true," Stephen began, approaching the issue from another angle, "then why didn't James Taylor bring suit? Why did he continue working for Cayson? I saw James in the front row at David's funeral! How did the two stay friends?" Questions flew out of Stephen's mouth as if he were cross-examining a witness, but Debra didn't flinch.

"Because James doesn't know the truth. He never did—and the guilt of it nearly ate my husband up in his last months. As you might've noticed, my husband was *especially* generous to the Taylor family. Yet in all these years, you never once thought to question why?

"We don't interfere with our client's finances on that level," Stephen replied, instinctively deflecting any liability. "We manage their legal needs."

"And how well do you manage their scandals? What if I also told you—"

"—Debra, you sound ridiculous!"

"I know where to find *all* the records." Debra said triumphantly "So unless you'd like me to release that information to the media, you might want to hear what I have to say. From start to finish."

Stephen rubbed his temples slowly as he thought the situation over. The conviction behind Debra words was apparent enough. He'd never heard of a Willie Taylor, but that didn't mean he wasn't listed in Cayson's books somewhere. And, knowing Big Jim, Stephen didn't doubt that he'd stepped out on his wife now and again. What

Stephen didn't know was how any of that was connected to Willie's death, and he didn't know how big of a scandal this could be for his firm. What Stephen did know was that above all else, he wanted to pass the firm on to his daughter and retire a wealthy man. If what Debra was saying was even half true, she could very well deprive him of that the golden years he longed for.

"Very well, Debra," Stephen started, purposefully slipping into the tone of familiarity he'd most often used with Debra over the years. "Start at the beginning. When did all of this occur?"

"The year was 1964."

Chapter 7

Summer, 1964

Montgomery, Alabama

"Ain't you tired of working?" James asked as he wiped sweat from his brow. He'd been laboring alongside Willie practically since sunup, and they were now at Willie's second job, gathering up the leftover pieces of lumber. "We worked all day, and you got me out here working after quitting time."

"Naw, I ain't tired yet, and you shouldn't be either. You younger than me." Willie laughed and picked up another bundle. "Besides, I never get tired of making money. An' these spent pieces of wood here, these are my gold. You came to the city to work, so complain less and work until there ain't no more to be done."

"Sure thing, boss," James joked as he saluted his constantly-moving cousin. The blazing summer sun, still high in the sky despite the hour, felt as if it were burning a hole in his neck. He tied his handkerchief around his collar before he went back to hauling and stacking.

James didn't normally work construction, and right now the muscles his arms were telling him as much. But, with his senior year of high school starting in September, he wanted to save up, so when David—his friend at Cayson Construction—had told him there were summer positions available, James jumped at the chance. Because David couldn't be seen playing favorites for a colored kid, he'd placed James with his cousin Willie—if anyone asked, Willie was the one who'd gotten him the job.

James hadn't exactly signed up for Willie's after-hours work, on top of his day job. New to the city, he'd hoped they would spend their evenings out on the town, but he also knew how important Willie's "side jobs" were to him. Family stuck with family, James knew that much. He reminded himself of that fact as his shoulders cried out in exhaustion.

To Willie, hard work was nothing new. For five years, he'd spent his days laboring for Cayson. His framing skills were second to none, but working for Cayson was just a way of making ends meet—each week he sent half his pay home to support his mother, who'd raised him on her own. On days when Cayson didn't give him a full day's work, Willie earned a few extra dollars by doing any type of general carpentry on his own. Beyond that, Willie had a true talent for woodworking—crafting, spinning, and polishing wood until he found the beauty within. His custom pieces were becoming increasingly known in the negro community. Willie spent every spare moment he could find working toward the day when he'd have his own business. He would achieve what his grandfather had not.

At twenty-four years old, Willie could now build anything that Papa Abe could've, and more. But Papa Abe, whose parents had been born enslaved, had spent his long life working for others. Jim Crow's shadow was heavy; despite his being the best carpenter in Alabama's Black Belt, the white man always got the credit.

Willie was the only grandchild ever interested in woodworking. While the other children were playing, Willie was right behind his Papa Abe, who'd built chairs, tables, alters, and mantles for his community in what little spare time he had. By the time Papa Abe died, Willie, at only fifteen years old, could carve, plane, and varnish almost as well as his grandfather.

"Since I been in Montgomery with you, we haven't had a day off," James complained as he moved more lumber. "We don't even work this hard in the fields back home."

For the first time all day, Willie stopped working. He dropped the piece of wood he was holding, walked over to his cousin, and looked him straight in the eye. Willie's expression turned grave, serious. "When you work in those fields, where does that money go? Who's getting the big paycheck?"

James took advantage of the pause and stopped to rest his weary arms for a few seconds. "It's always the landowner, I know that." James shrugged. "So what?"

"And when we working for Cayson, who's profiting from our sweat?"

"I know Big Jim's the one making money hand over fist," James replied. "That's just the way it is. Those who got, get."

"You may think the money we earn from Big Jim is enough, but when you have real responsibilities, you'll know better." Willie tapped the side of James' forehead. "What we're doing right now, this is for me. This is what *I* want to do, and I'm doing it the way I want it done. One day, this here is *all* I'll be doing. I'll be getting that big paycheck."

James reached down and picked up the smallest piece of wood he could see. "An' what you saving these little pieces for, anyway?"

"All pieces of wood ain't good for everything, but every piece of wood is good for something." Willie winked. "Some smaller pieces become decoration, but most I use for reinforcement. Anything I make is strong and it lasts. That's what I'm building my reputation on, that's why I'm gon' have my own shop before long."

"Cousin, these white folks ain't gon' let you do that," James said provokingly, trying to stretch out their break as long as he could. He wasn't lazy, but he *was* tired.

"What you mean they ain't gon' let me?" Willie shot back, although there was laughter in his eyes. "I've been getting quite a few jobs from colored folks all over town. That's how I got my truck."

"And a sorry looking truck it is," James teased. "Ugly as sin itself. We've got to get you some style. My first car gon' be the finest ride on the road."

"Pretty ain't my concern. I saved three years for that truck, all from my own jobs. It runs good, it's dependable. It may not be much to look at, but that pickup is my freedom. Now I can get to any job, anywhere, with all my supplies. You gon' hire someone who can't come to you? Or show up without tools?"

"Alright, alright," laughed James. "I'm with you now. Jus' don't be surprised when that ugly thing runs the ladies off."

"Any woman worth having wants a hard-working man. I ain't worried none on that account." Wille teased.

The two laughed together easily. Though he didn't show it much, Willie was glad to have his cousin by his side. He'd missed being with the folks he grew up with. Even if

James could only stay for a few months, his presence would make summer's hard, hot work that much lighter.

After a moment, Willie's expression turned somber again as he spotted an unfamiliar brown sedan crawling down the path to the build site. "Stay up," he warned. It was dangerous to be unaware, and, for black men living in the South, laughter come as brief as sunshine in winter.

As the car rumbled closer, Willie moved in front of James. He'd promised Uncle George and Aunt Thelma that nothing would happen to their son, and he was aiming to keep his word.

The middle-aged man in the car rolled his window all the way down. "You're the one who's working on this porch here?" he asked, as he stuck out his hand for Willie to shake.

"Yes, sir. I'm Willie." He shook the driver's hand out of politeness, thankful to see the warm brown of the man's skin. "Willie Taylor."

"Then you're the man I've been looking for. They say you're pretty good with wood."

"Well, I try to do my best, yes sir."

"I'm Earl Roberson. I live just a few doors down the way," the man said as he pointed Eastward.

"Good to know you, sir. This here is my cousin, James." Willie nodded toward his cousin. "He's working with me for the summer till he goes back to school."

Mr. Roberson turned to James. "Nice to meet you, son." James, still a bit shy of strangers, only nodded respectfully in reply.

"Now Willie, I believe you did some work for a friend of mine here in Washington Park," Mr. Roberson said. "A nice toy box for his daughter."

"Yes sir, that was Mr. Mitchell. Built that about a month ago, I reckon." Willie smiled as he remembered the curved top of the maple toy chest. "My granddaddy taught me all he knew 'bout working with wood. Out on his old farm."

"So you're a country boy, huh?" He laughed.

"Yes, sir." Willie puffed up a little. "Born and raised. My cousin and I stay in town for the week, but we're home 'bout every weekend helping our mamas."

"Alright then," Earl Roberson slapped the side of his sedan as he smiled. "Do you expect you could make a mantel for our fireplace? My wife's been after me for weeks, and I'm afraid I've let it go a mite too long. She wants it ready for a party we're having next Sunday. I'd be obliged if you could make her happy."

Willie's eyes lit up. He could make a mantel in his sleep—it was his favorite kind of woodworking, and his most praised. An image of the piece he wanted to carve had already jumped into his mind. "Yes, sir. I'd be glad to," Willie beamed. "I can sketch it out the mantle first, if that would suit. An' then I'll make it real nice for you."

"Good." Earl grinned back. "And you can have it installed by Friday, in the evening? I'll compensate you well for your efforts, son."

Willie thought for a moment, calculating his time. To make the quality piece that he envisioned on time would be a push. Willie needed another day to finish the porch on this job site, leaving exactly one week to complete the new request.

Willie looked over at James, who shrugged his shoulders, and then over at Mr. Roberson's expectant grin. He knew his muscles would regret it later, but Willie couldn't resist the lure of crafting wood. "I'll make that sketch for you tonight, sir, then call on you at home after work tomorrow, if that's convenient."

"Here's my number." Earl extended a card with his information printed neatly across it. "Our home address is on the back. I'll tell my wife to expect you. I may not be home, but you can go over the plans with her. Please her and you'll be pleasing me."

"Yes, sir." Willie nodded before he traced the black letters of the business card. "I'll get to you right away. And do give Mr. Mitchell my regards for the referral."

Chapter 8

"I've never been so glad to see this place in my life." James patted his hand on his grumbling stomach. "I'm ready to wash up, eat some of Rosa Mae's good cooking, an' call it a night."

"I'm a hungry myself," Willie admitted as he parked his well-worked, dependable truck.

"Lord, I know she got that smothered liver ready." James rubbed his hands together in anticipation. "I can smell it all the way out here."

"Calm down, cousin."

"I can't. Rosa Mae is a fine cook. How'd you come to find this ol' place, anyhow?"

"I found it just like everybody else. This here is a boarding house for working men, an' every working colored man in this town knows Rosa Mae's," he answered. "Even more so 'cause of her café. Hot dinner every night, included in the rent. Can't beat that."

"Naw, you sure can't," said James, trying to sound worldly. The truth was, before this summer, he'd never spent a night anywhere other than his own home.

"You just lucky she let you double with me this summer. She only allowed it on account of me being here these last four years. Plus, you meet her other rules—you know how she is 'bout all that stuff."

Before even inquiring about a room at Rosa Mae's, a person had to meet her basic requirements. Not a soul darkened her doorstep if they didn't meet the expectations proclaimed in her faded windowsill sign: "Colored Working MEN Only." Rosa Mae firmly adhered to every word, no exceptions. She surrounded herself with men in every way she knew how. There wasn't a woman walking the Earth that Rosa Mae Brown wanted in her midst, and that included the woman who'd birthed her. But she did love every kind of working man ever made, and every man who'd ever received Rosa Mae's attention loved her right back.

Which didn't mean she was soft on her boarders. Any man who wanted a room had to prove he had a job. Didn't matter what kind of job, really, as long as he drew a paycheck every week. Brown's Boarding House didn't allow freebies, and once Rosa Mae had slashed a man's face for trying to run out on his rent. Since then, that was another thing the working men of Montgomery all knew; Rosa Mae's switchblade Sally was the only lady allowed in her life, and Rosa Mae was never without her.

"Listen, wait up," Willie called out just as his cousin's hand landed on the handle of the café door.

James turned with the pout of a toddler on his face. "Aw, come on, not now—I'm tryin' to get to this food."

Willie stepped closer. "You remember what I told you 'bout Rosa Mae?"

"Yeah, yeah." James bobbed his head from side to side as he repeated Wille's warning. "If she asks me to help with the furniture in her bedroom, don't go."

"That's right. I expect she's tried that line on every man who ever walked through this door," Willie replied. "An' I believe it worked on most of them. But not on me, and not on you either. I don't care how fine her behind is."

"Those hips could knock a man out, too. Don't forget that." A sly smile crept across James' face as he spoke.

"I'm serious, James. We was raised better than that. No matter what she says or how she says it, don't go."

"I don't know why," James laughed. "I can show her how a real man does it."

Wille couldn't contain the laughter that erupted from his belly. "That woman would put you to bed like the baby you are. She almost twice your age, and she got twice your know-how. She would have you shouting for Jesus and your mama in less than a minute flat."

The stony expression glued to Willie's face gave him pause. James lifted an eyebrow as he asked, "Is that supposed to scare me?"

"I told Uncle George I'd take good care of you, and that's what I'm doing. You too young to risk getting a grown woman into the family way."

James placed a hand over his heart, "I promise, okay? Now can we go eat?"

The two walked through the door and right into Rosa Mae Brown. "I was just about to lock up, you late tonight," she said as she looked up one cousin and down the other. "Come on in here and get you something good to put your mouth on."

The two followed the switch of Rosa Mae's hips to the counter, then took seats a few stools down from LeRoy. He was a regular at the café, but he didn't live in the attached boarding house. The man mostly drank, sometimes worked, and he always found Rosa Mae. LeRoy's love for her was fierce, and to his mind any boarder was automatically his rival. Willie was even more of a target because of the lightness of his complexion.

"Hey, Old Yellow," LeRoy sneered.

"I already told you my name ain't Old Yellow. It's Willie." He glared right back at LeRoy. "Get it right or I'll throw you out myself." Willie would joke about many things, but his family, his work, and his skin were not on the list.

LeRoy grumbled. "Pretty yellow nigger."

The two men rose from their stools at the same time, staring straight at each other. Neither of them blinked. James rose slowly from his seat to back up his cousin.

"Not tonight LeRoy!" Rosa Mae slid around the counter and between the two men. "You know his damn name."

"Yeah. Young yellow," he spat. Willie reached past Rosa Mae to swipe at LeRoy, but she smacked his hand away.

It's time for you to get yourself moving," Rosa Mae commanded. "You ain't brought a nothing but a cup of coffee since you been here. I told you—if you ain't buying, you ain't staying. Willie here is my boarder, a *paying* boarder."

"Not you or this high yellow nigger gon' tell me when to git," LeRoy huffed. "I go when I'm damn well ready to go."

When LeRoy didn't move, Rosa Mae did. In one fluid movement, she retrieved Sally from her bosom and flipped the blade open. "I said go!"

At the sound of the blade clicking open, LeRoy dropped his bravado and began slowing walking away. He moved toward the door without letting his back ever see Rosa Mae.

"I ain't ever coming here again!" he shouted when his back hit the door.

"You'll be back, and when you do come, bring some damn money," she sneered. "I can't stand me a broke man."

He finally turned, exited, and stomped outside. This wasn't the first time Rosa Mae had kicked LeRoy out, and Willie wondered if she really would slash him one of these days.

She carefully folded Sally up and slipped the blade back into its special hiding place. "Sorry about that, boys," she said with a smile. "I got your food right here." She stepped over to the stove and quickly put together two plates of smothered liver and rice.

James' mouth hung open, but it wasn't because of the food. He was amazed at how Rosa Mae, petite as she was, seemed to grow three feet when she was brandishing Sally, but then effortlessly slid right back into sweet and sexy. Maybe Willie had been right; maybe this woman knew a thing or two he didn't.

"How's that side job I set up for you?" Rosa Mae asked as she placed the plates in front of the two hungry men.

"Going jus' about as good as a job can go, thank you." Wille's eyes brightened with excitement as he tucked his napkin into his collar. "That porch is coming up right nice, if I do say so myself." He reached into the front pocket of his pants and pulled out a roll of one-dollar bills. "And I got your fee for you too. I wasn't 'specting to get paid till tomorrow, but payday come early."

Rosa Mae licked her thumb, straightened the tip of each bill, then counted them softly to herself. "You're welcome." She looked up and sparkled a smile at Willie. "This is why I only allow men here. Women don't earn, they can't do nothing for me."

"That's where you and I differ, Miss Brown," James piped up, wiping his mouth. "There's a whole lot a woman can do for me."

Rosa Mae licked her lips. "You better watch what you say until you ready to watch what I do, sweet baby."

Willie elbowed his cousin in warning. With a startled jump, James shook his head and decided to put it his focus on something he could handle: his dinner.

Laughing, Rosa Mae leaned over the counter and turned her attention to Willie, "How much more you got on that job?"

"Not much. Should be finished by tomorrow afternoon, I reckon. Cayson only needs us in the morning." He swallowed his mouthful of rice before continuing. "An' now I got another job lined up with a man named Earl Roberson."

"Oh yeah, I know Mr. Roberson." Rosa Mae nodded. "He got a business of some sort over by the post office, and his brother got a good government job over at city hall, sweeping up and such. They good people, but just don't you get caught up in any of Roberson's Civil Rights nonsense.

Do your work, nothing more, an' he will pay you just fine."

She walked over to her cash register and opened it. She took half of the bills Willie had given her and put them in the till.

"About Cayson tomorrow… I intended to tell you your boss called," Rosa Mae recalled as she picked up a slip of paper that she'd taped to the register. "David said there's a delay with the lumber shipment. He won't need either of you at all tomorrow."

"Well that does free you up some," James said with his mouth full. Maybe we can finish that porch early an' have time to start on that mantel."

"That would work out just fine," Willie mumbled, enjoying his food. "I'd much rather be on my own jobs, anyway."

"And in the meantime," Rosa Mae broke in, "I'll start nosing around for another side job for you. For my usual fee, of course."

Willie nearly dropped his fork from glee. Word of mouth was everything in Montgomery, and with Rosa Mae's mouth now working for him, he was sure to be busy every day this summer. Plus, he didn't have to worry: Rosa Mae knew how to make inquiries to the right people in the right way. "Thank you kindly," he said through a smile.

Rosa Mae slid over to James, who hadn't let his fork leave his hand. She leaned the bounty of her breast over the counter, then wiped the corner of the teenager's clean-shaven face with her thumb. "You had a little something right there," she explained in a honied tone to a shocked James.

All but frozen, James marveled at the beauty before him. It was the first time Rosa Mae had touched him liked that, and she was now so close to him that he could see the place between her firm breasts where she kept Sally.

"James," she said sweetly as she adjusted her bosom. "Maybe tonight you can come on up to my room tonight and help me… move some furniture."

Chapter 9

David scanned the line of men standing in the outer office. Each man had come to receive his reward for a long week of work: his paycheck.

"Afternoon Mr. Cayson, sir." One after another of his laborers greeted him as he walked through the outer office and into his private space. He nodded at each of the men's familiar, dark faces as he passed by. Usually, David personally visited Cayson's sites to hand out checks, but on any Friday without a build, his men came to him.

Although Cayson Construction did have white employees, mostly managers and foremen, nearly all of Cayson's laborers were colored. To avoid race mixing, white men got paid on Wednesdays, negro men on Fridays. It had been that way ever since David could remember—well before he'd dropped out of high school to join Big Jim's side. He'd started by running errands and doing general office jobs, and along the way Big Jim had taught him something about every aspect of management. And now, at only twenty-two years old, David was running the Montgomery office, while Big Jim spent most of his time at the Selma office.

"We'll get started in a minute," David told the line of waiting men as he disappeared into his office. He closed the door behind him, opened the safe, then buzzed his secretary. Before she'd even entered the room, he'd already re-closed the heavy metal vault and given its sturdy combination lock a good spin.

"Are you ready, sir?" his secretary asked as she stepped through the door.

"I am. Let's get these boys paid," he replied loudly enough for the waiting men to hear. "Same as always, Constance. Leave the door open."

David sat down in his leather chair and grinned as Constance went back to her desk. "Treat your workers right, but never let them forget who signs their paychecks, son,"

Big Jim had often told him. David took this advice to heart, and payroll was the job he enjoyed the most; not one Cayson employee in all of Montgomery, white or colored, could receive his check without David first approving his hours and pay rate. He enjoyed watching as each man signed for his check, and an even greater pleasure ran through him as each looked into his office, tipped his hat, and muttered, "Thank you, Mr. Cayson."

James was the last man to pick up his check, which was unusual. With all his youthful energy, he'd been at the head of the payroll line, whether on a site or here in the office, every week since he'd started the job. David couldn't but help notice that James was without his cousin, too; he hadn't seen one without the other all summer.

"James," David called. "Come on in here a spell." James peeked into his envelope, made sure his check was inside, then headed into the office.

"I sure do love getting a paycheck every week, David," he said as he stepped into the office. "I work at least this hard at home, but I never saw me a dime on the farm."

David laughed, but then he added, "You have to call me Mr. Cayson at work, mind."

James tipped his hat as a sort of apology. "It's just you and me here, though. I'll be more careful on site."

"Fair enough," agreed David. "Now tell me, have you found yourself a city gal yet?"

James smiled mischievously at the thought of Rosa Mae's bosom. "Can't say as I have, though I might have one or two prospects. But mostly I'm too busy for that kind of thing."

"Well, I suppose that's what it is to be a working man," David replied affably before changing the subject. "I was hoping to talk to Willie this afternoon, where is he? Why didn't he come for his pay?"

Although David never admitted it to anyone, he had trouble reading the plans for Cayson's projects—measurements and angles weren't his strongest suit. For years he'd been relying on Willie, who read blueprints as easily as children's rhymes, to fill the gap; this afternoon he'd expected some help on specs for an upcoming build. As always, David planned to go home to Big Jim, pretending he'd figured it all out on his own.

"Well, since we ain't working at all today, he decided to finish up a side job," James explained. "You know he can't sit still for long."

Anger surged through David, although he was careful to keep smiling—Willie should've told him to his face about any outside work. A side job was bad enough, but not even bothering to pick up his check was very nearly an insult. If Willie was holding back, there had to be a reason for it: a reason David now wanted to know.

"In fact," James continued innocently, "I should be getting along. I'm supposed to meet Willie and help him."

"I was just about to close up and head home," David said as he formulated a plan. "I can give you a ride." Although he hated the idea of pumping childhood friend for information, he knew he had an obligation to his Daddy— and to the company—to keep on top of all his employees.

"That's mighty kind of you," James beamed. "I don't mind tell you, my dogs are barking. I'm still not used these work boots. I bought 'em special for the summer."

"Go on, then, I'll meet you at the truck. Bring that box of files out for me, would you?" David reached over and patted his old friend on the shoulder with an orchestrated warmth.

Thankful for the ride, James picked up the file box in the corner. It twice as heavy as he'd expected, and he had trouble getting a firm hold on it.

"He'd better not cross that line," David hissed under his breath without realizing it.

"What was that, did you say something?" James asked, balancing the box on one knee as he adjusted his grip.

"Nothing, nothing," David deflected. "Thanks much for taking that to the truck for me."

Good employee or not, James' cousin or not, if Willie was taking construction jobs from white folks, that would be a blatant sign of disrespect. Yet he couldn't think of another reason why Willie wouldn't have come to him. David tried to calm himself before jumping to conclusions, but it seemed he'd already leaped halfway there.

In the parking lot, James was waiting by David's truck, still holding the heavy file box. "I expect you want this up front with you, so the top don't blow off. The cabin's locked, though."

"Good thinking," replied David as he pulled out his keys. James slid the box into the front seat, and then, without a second thought, he turned to hop onto the flatbed.

"You can stay up here with me, if you want," David offered casually.

Knowing colored men had died for far less, James rubbed his ear as he made sure he'd heard correctly. Even in the city, there were rules to Southern life: negroes did not ride in front with whites.

"Like you said, it's just us," David encouraged. "It'll be fine."

A shadow passed over James' face. For the first time, it dawned on him: he and David may have been friends as kids, but as adults—with work and color between them— they were now something in-between. James honestly didn't know if he should follow David's instructions or find himself a comfortable position on the flatbed. Either one could cause him problems.

"Look, there's plenty of room," David urged, pretending not to notice James' discomfort. "I'll just slide this box into the middle seat."

"Well, I appreciate it," James finally relented. The sun was still high in the late afternoon sky, "Cayson Construction" was clearly printed on the cabin's side, and the drive would only take ten minutes. He'd trust his friend. He climbed into the cabin, thankful that the file box separated them.

"Where should I drop you off?" David asked as he pulled out of the parking lot.

"On Davis Street, if you don't mind. In Washington Park. I don't expect that's too far out of your way."

David breathed a silent sigh. Washington Park was Montgomery's negro neighborhood—Willie hasn't crossed the line, at least not yet. To hide his relief, he reached down and turned on the radio. He fiddled with the dial for a moment, then switched the knob off abruptly.

"I guess Wille stays pretty busy, huh?" David asked as casually as he could.

"He just can't keep himself from the wood," James chuckled. "Ever since we were kids. Even on Sundays. Sometimes I'd have to beg him just to take me down to the creek fishing."

"So he's been working another job for a while now?" David asked, pushing just a little bit more.

Suddenly uncomfortable, James wiped his brow to give himself a moment. "I don't know about that… But you know we're dedicated to Cayson. Work for you and Big Jim comes first."

The air around them stilled.

After a moment, David replied, "No doubt it does— it's hard to pass up steady pay." To ease the tension even more, he spoke his next words in an easy tone. "I guess I can't expect to keep all Willie's talents for myself."

"Only if you gave him twelve hours a day, seven days a week," James said, cracking a smile. "That might tucker him out just enough."

"If I had it, I'd give it. But tell me, how you like working with us?" David asked, changing the subject. James had given him all he needed to know, for now at least.

"I like it," he answered with an excited relief. It was much easier to talk about himself. "Being around men all day, grown men—not the kids at school. An' I like the city, too. Before this summer, I ain't been here but for a few times."

"I'll tell you what. I've seen you out there—you work hard, and you get along with my other guys. As soon as you graduate, you can come back and start with us full-time." He looked over at James. "I promise you that as a friend."

Even James knew passing up a job offer required respectful words. He gnawed on his bottom lip for a moment.

"I thank you, that's awful kind of you. I'd be happy to work summers, but right now I'm thinking of going to Tuskegee."

"Tuskegee! College!" David laughed from a deep place in his gut. "Why would you waste your time doing that? I'm offering you a paying job, starting the day after you graduate. Four extra years of school means nothing but bills."

James shrugged. "It's worth a try." More and more negros were going to college all the time, making Tuskegee seem like a real possibility—especially since he had always kept his grades up. Construction would always be an option, but college was a one-shot chance.

The two rode in silence for the last few minutes of the drive. James tried to think of something more to say, but he was distracted: David drove as if he rode with negroes in his front seat every day.

"You can put me off here, if you would. Willie's just yonder," James said, pointing.

Willie heard the truck approaching. Not many things caught him off guard—he tried to plan ahead and think things through. He prided himself on being one step ahead of most, but when he looked up from his level and saw James in the front seat of David's truck, he felt more than ten steps behind.

"What the…?" Willie muttered, squinting his eyes hard as the truck rolled closer. He concluded that his eyes still worked, but he didn't want to believe what he was seeing. He'd taken many a precaution to keep his side jobs quiet: working on his own didn't mean he was doing anything wrong, exactly, but Willie knew a colored man making his own way would never sit right to any white man who felt he was the way-maker.

With a slight smile on his face, James stepped down from the blissfully ignorant of what he'd just done. Willie all but kicked himself; he'd never exactly told James to keep his side jobs a secret, but then he'd never once thought he would need to say as much aloud.

David, still perched high up in his truck, glowered at Willie. Trouble was brewing, Willie knew that much. Just how bad this really was would remain to be seen.

"Hey, captain, reporting for duty," James chided as he approached his silently-fuming cousin. Willie could only hope that James wasn't as ignorant as seemed. "But now that I'm here, I'm thinking don't need me at all—look like this porch is 'most finished," James continued.

Once the tail end of David's truck had turned the corner, Willie grabbed James by the shoulders, pulled him close, and yanked him up by the collar of his shirt. "What the hell you brought him here for?" he shouted, nearly forgetting that the young man in his grip was his own blood. "The last thing I need is David knowing 'bout my work!"

"But I… I jus'… He offered me a ride," sputtered James in his shock. Willie had never laid his hands on him in anger before, and he'd never seen so much fiery anger in his cousin's eyes.

"Three years I been working on my own, and not once did the boss-man ever find out! Do you know what you just done?" Flecks of spit flew from Willie's mouth and straight onto James' face.

"Don't be mad," James pleaded apologetically. "It's jus' David. We known him since we were coming up."

"You don't understand!" Willie shook his cousin hard before he let him go. "You got to think! Friend or no friend, there are *rules*. Even you know that!"

"I didn't mean nothing by it," James apologized sheepishly.

Unsure of what to do with himself, Willie started pacing. "Maybe you too young yet for city life," he muttered, "if you ain't got sense enough to keep the white man from knowing what he don't need to know."

"That's not fair "I'm only a year younger than you was when you first started! An' I ain't done nothing but keep a few miles off my feet."

"What did he get out of you?" Willie snapped.

"Get?" James cried, honestly confused. "I carried a box out to the truck for him, if that's what you mean."

Willie balled his fists in frustration. "I mean when he asked 'bout me. What did you tell him, how *much* did you tell him?"

"I told him Cayson comes first, but that you're one to keep moving," answered James honestly enough. "David would never betray you," he added, almost pleading. "You know that. He's only ever wanted what's best for me—and for you, too."

Willie couldn't stand still. He started pacing again, striding back and forth between his tool bag and the curb. "Three years building up a reputation. The right way. The *quiet* way. Cousin, I pray you right about David, or we could

both be out of a job!"

Chapter 10

Willie finished polishing the mantel with great care. It had turned out to be one of his finest pieces. Taking a step back, he admired his craftsmanship. Sometimes he amazed even himself. "Perfect!" he declared. He pressed his fingertips to his lips, made a kissing sound, then flung his hand into the air just like he'd seen Italian men do in the movies.

"I told you it looked good a long time ago," James said from his spot on the grass. He'd grown bored with watching Willie rub and pamper the mantle endlessly. His cousin kept fussing over every detail, which kept had James away from what he really wanted to do: go home to the farm for the weekend.

"I heard what you said," Willie responded halfheartedly as he walked around his work. He needed it to be perfect from every angle. "I jus' didn't think it was right, yet."

"This job could've been done *hours* ago." James stood up and moved closer to his cousin. "Now we have to wait to go back home, an' I'll miss dinner with my people. I won't see Mama 'til tomorrow."

"I tell you what, I'll—" Willie stopped mid-sentence, took his rag from his back pocket, and wiped the right corner of the mantle another time.

James grabbed the rag. "Stop. It's perfect already. There ain't nothing else you can do to it."

Willie smiled. "Sorry, it's jus'… there was a spot of… never mind. As I was 'bout to say, I'll take you home in the morning, real early. I'll have you on back on the farm in time for your mama's breakfast."

"You talking just to hear the sound of your voice," James scoffed.

"Honest." Willie put his hand up like he was about to testify in court. "Now you get this truck loaded so we can get to bed early tonight. I need to talk to the Robersons before we get to installing this. I'll be out in a spell."

"Alright, jus' don't get lost," James cautioned as he began gathering the few loose tools in the yard.

Willie had spent most of the last four hours in the Roberson's back yard finishing their new mantel. Mrs. Roberson had approved the sketch the moment she'd seen it, and Willie had spent most of his evenings over the past week crafting that design to perfection. And although he'd feared David was going to cut his hours or outright fire him, things at Cayson had blown over with nothing more than a few tense, awkward looks between the two men.

He walked up to the back porch and knocked respectfully at the screen door. The couple was sitting in their kitchen sipping coffee and waiting. "Mr. and Mrs. Roberson," Willie began, removing his hat, "it's done."

Janice Roberson hopped up from the kitchen table with the speed of an Olympic sprinter. "I sure am excited," she called over her shoulder to her husband as she practically flew past Willie.

"Slow down, dear," Mr. Roberson chuckled. "That mantle won't run away."

"I do hope you like it, ma'am," Willie called as she practically skipped toward his creation. He started down the porch steps after her.

"Oh, it's perfect!" squealed Mrs. Roberson as she walked around the mantle, which was still laying across Willie's sawhorses. "It's just what I imagined. And the stain is the perfect color for my front room."

"Well it does look nice from back here," Mr. Roberson teased. His wife had moved so quickly that he was just now coming down the porch steps.

"I already know which photographs will suit it best," she said as she ran a hand across the piece. "The one with Brenda and my daddy will go right in the middle."

"This *is* nicely put together, son," Mr. Roberson said as he examined Willie's work more closely. "Simple and elegant, just like my wife wanted." He nodded as he ran his eyes along the grain of the wood. "How long you been doing this type of work? Not just carpentry, I mean making custom pieces."

"Just 'bout all my life." Willie beamed, excited at the couple's approval. "My granddaddy taught me building and beautifying at the same time. An' I did enjoy this job in particular, sir. Clean and elegant lets the beauty of the wood shine through on its own."

"Gentlemen, if you'll excuse me, I'm going to gather up my pictures. Willie, I expect you'll be installing your fine work before you leave us this evening?"

"Of course, ma'am. My cousin and I will take care of that for you. Won't take but a few minutes."

Mr. Roberson waited until his wife was out of earshot. "Son, you could make a good living making custom pieces—if you were working for yourself."

"That's what I'm aiming for someday, sir. A shop of my own, offering some mix of carpentry and custom." Willie shook his head. "But right now, I got to keep my day job. I got my mama back home to help take care of."

"Young man," Mr. Roberson placed a hand on Willie's shoulder, "you've got to believe in yourself. This is the second piece of yours that I've seen, and both are exemplary."

Willie's whole face lit up. "Thank you. I do believe my work speaks for itself, but that ain't all it takes to run a business. I work my side jobs jus' like I work with wood. It takes great care and time to get things right. Same thing for building a business. I'm gon' take my time."

Mr. Roberson's expression slid from admiration to serious. "Now *is* the time. Things are changing around here faster than you can blink. Move with the water or drown being still, that's what I always say." He nodded his head as if agreeing with himself. "Son, if you don't remember anything else I tell you, remember this: working for a white man will always keep you living from paycheck to paycheck."

Willie searched Mr. Roberson's eyes, and he saw that the older man was giving him some well-intended advice. Willie smiled at that. He could count on one hand the number of times a successful man had encouraged him.

"I do believe you are right, sir. Just because I don't hop into business for myself today, don't mean I won't." With those words, Willie stuck out his hand for Mr. Roberson to shake.

Palming the young carpenter's hand, Earl Roberson extended an invitation that he rarely offered. "I tell you what," he said as he clapped his free hand against Willie's shoulder, "Come by my house Sunday evening for that party I mentioned. We'll be celebrating my daughter's birthday."

Willie raised a perplexed eyebrow. "That's kind of you, sir, but I don't expect it's proper to attend a party for a young lady I've not been introduced to as yet."

Mr. Roberson laughed heartily. "Good country manners!" he cried as he clapped Willie on the shoulder again. "You've been raised up right."

"Willie!" Mrs. Roberson called from the porch door. "Your cousin's in the front room, double-checking the measurements. He asked that I tell you."

"Thank you, ma'am," Willie called back, smiling as he lifted his hat. Three weeks ago, James never would've even thought to double-check specs. His cousin was learning.

"Now son, this isn't just a birthday party. There will be other guests, but there are some men in particular I'd like to introduce you to, all business owners in the community.

We meet on the regular. The party is… Well, I'd do anything for my sweet girl, but it's also good cover. Keeps some eyes off us."

Willie reached down and zipped up his tool bag. "I don't know about that," he deflected as he started walking toward the house. "If you'll excuse me, I best see to my cousin." He wasn't sure he wanted to be involved in Earl Roberson's civil rights activities. The movement had proven dangerous for many negroes already.

Mr. Roberson stepped in stride with Willie all the way up the porch steps. "Nonsense." He opened the screen door. "We'll have food and drinks, and a cake for my Brenda. Regrettable to conduct business on the Lord's day, I understand, but we do have to take precautions. But all in all, I'll be old-fashioned fun, and you may even gain a customer or two."

The prospect of new clients was too alluring. The more people he knew—providing they could be discreet—the better for his business. "You know what, sir?" Willie paused in the middle of the kitchen, turning to face Mr. Roberson. "I'd be glad to come, providing you recommend my services personally. My cousin and I gon' be at home tomorrow, but we could drive back direct after Sunday services."

Earl Roberson's eyes flashed with excitement. "A recommendation, by all mean. Will do, young man, will do!" He reached into his pocket, pulled out a fold of bills, and gave Willie his payment along with a fair tip.

Rolling the money in his palm, Willie felt like things in his life were about to change for the better. "Thank you, Mr. Roberson. Tell your wife that I thank her too. Now let me get that mantle installed for you proper."

"Bring that young cousin of yours with you, too," said the older man added as he walked Willie the few remaining steps to the front room. "He's a good worker. No telling where he could go in life. We'll see you both here on Sunday. Five-thirty, don't be late!"

Chapter 11

The drive home dragged on for what seemed like an eternity to Willie, and James had slept for most of it. Willie didn't mind that, though—his younger cousin has earned his rest. They'd both worked hard during the week, and they'd gotten up with the first rays of the sun this morning.

Stretching his arms as he woke, James yawned. "Finally, we're almost home."

"Yeah, no thanks to you. I could've let you ride in the flatbed, an' at least put me something pretty up here to look at."

"Cousin, I'm the prettiest negro you know." Laughing, he rubbed his hand across the scraggly hairs blooming on his smooth face.

"I could've left you at Rosa Mae's and took another job, pretty boy." Willie was only half joking.

"Naw," James drawled. "You owed me this trip. We didn't go home last weekend, an' I been promising my mama I wouldn't miss two weeks in a row."

"I know, I know." Willie shook his head. "But when it comes time to speak on me, you be sure to remember that I'm the best cousin in the world. I had to get myself up at five-thirty this morning jus' to get you home in time for your mama's breakfast."

"Yeah, and I'll just make it—barely." He looked at his watch. "If you can get up every day to go to work, then you can get up to get me home."

"Spoken like a true mama's boy," Willie laughed. "But honestly, you should be just as serious as I am about your work. You're a natural. You picked up skills in a few weeks that takes most men a whole year to get a proper handle on."

"Naw," James said again. "I'm gon' give college a shot first. I tol' you that already."

"Well now, I can't argue with that. A college education is a fine option. If you go that route, you can count on me. Can't much help with tuition, but you'll have yourself other expenses—I'll chip in where I can.

James smiled widely, grateful for his older cousin's support. "I do appreciate that, but I expect you won't have to. Construction during the summers will see me through."

Willie laughed. His cousin still had no sense of just how expensive living in the world could be. He decided to skip the lecture for the moment, though, since they were only a few yards from James' home.

"Alright, college boy, we're here. Go on, git. Give my regards to your daddy and a kiss to your mama."

James grabbed the brown paper bag filled with his belongings. The weight of his clothes had poked a hole through one side. A sock fell out and landed on the floor of the cabin.

"James, you making some money now. You need something decent to carry your clothes in." Willie poked at the tattered brown bag, making another hole. "This thing is shameful. Your clothes be tryin' to run away to freedom!"

"Don't I know it," he replied as he tried to cover both the holes and his embarrassment.

"Don't throw your money away on nothing this weekend," Willie instructed. I'm taking you shopping when we back in Montgomery. You can buy you a suitcase."

"You're right. I'm a working man now, I should have a few decent things. I *am* tryin' to save, but spending on need ain't the same as spending for fun."

"That's exactly right," Willie advised. "An' don't forget to bring back something nice from your closet, too. We got that party tomorrow, and you need to dress like you was going to services."

"Don't you worry I'll be dressed to impress!" boasted James as he stepped out of the truck.

"I'll be back directly after lunch tomorrow to pick you up." Willie yelled from the window as he put the truck in reverse and started backing down the dirt road. "Two o'clock, be ready!"

§

Willie froze as he pulled up to his mama's house. That other truck, the one he'd seen parked there so many times, kept him locked in his own truck with the engine running. He had to take five minutes to collect himself, revving his engine occasionally. He hoped the motor's roar would alert his mother and her guest to his arrival. Because as much as he wanted to see his mama, he couldn't stand the man who came calling whenever he had a particular itch to scratch.

He walked up to his mother's screened-in porch and took a deep breath. Steadying his hand, he placed it against the cool metal doorknob, reminding himself not to let his emotions get the better of him.

Unease rolled through his stomach. For years, neighbors whispered about the man in the truck who came calling on his mother, Rita. Everyone knew, but never said outright, that the driver of the truck, Big Jim Cayson, was Willie's father. That's why he was so light-skinned, not dark and smooth like his cousins.

Big Jim came around when Big Jim felt like it. He'd park his truck in front of the house, find his way inside Willie's mother, then walk out the front door without so much a mumbling a word to his own son. Growing up, Willie never got the chance to play ball, go fishing, or sit in the barbershop with his father, and he resented it. Sometimes Uncle George would pick him up from school or take him for a soda pop, but it wasn't the same.

The sounds of a squeaky headboard and his mother's moans filled Willie's memory. He never knew when he'd come home to Big Jim, a married man, stepping into his mama's bedroom. And it was just as true today as it was twenty years ago. Why his mother allowed it, he didn't understand. Her beauty was famous across Lowndes County, yet she'd never wanted a man—she'd pushed many away many a time. But Big Jim stayed, year after year.

Sometimes Willie wondered how he'd ever been born in the first place. He remembered too well the three nights, years apart, when his mother had doubled over the toilet with sickness, and then lay hurt and bleeding in her bed. One time, infection had seeped through her body—she was sick and shivering from fever for days. If Willie, still in short pants, hadn't gone for help and convinced Aunt Thelma to take her to the clinic for colored women, he was sure he would've lost his mama. What they lost instead was the little money they had saved—half for the appointment and half to keep the doctor quiet.

Things became even more complicated as Willie grew older. Just when he was about to become man enough to challenge Big Jim, his mama had pulled him into the kitchen—where all their serious conversations started—and told him he would be working at Cayson Construction. She'd considered it good news, and Willie, fresh out of high school, was in no position to turn down a paying job, not when so many colored men were out of work.

During those first few weeks on the job, a part of Willie had hoped that Big Jim would acknowledge him as his son. But he never did, and it stung all the more knowing that he was Big Jim's only child; Big Jim's wife Martha was barren. When David, Martha's nephew who Big Jim *did* accept as a son, had taken over the Montgomery office, Willie breathed a sigh of relief.

At last he gathered his resolve. "Mama," Wille called out as poked his head through the door with his eyes closed. He was afraid to open them, too afraid to witness something no son should ever see.

"Baby, what you doing here so early for? I wasn't expecting you till later this morning." His mother's voice had the same sing-song quality that it always had. It instantly soothed him.

Opening the door widely, Rita squinted as the morning sunlight caressed her smooth face. She smiled at her son, genuinely happy to see him. "Come on in, but I do need myself a minute," she said before scurrying down the hall and into her bedroom.

"You know James wanted to get to his mama," Willie called out as he stepped inside. He walked down the long hall and straight into the kitchen, averting his eyes as he passed his mother's bedroom. He would give her time to compose herself.

A few minutes later, Rita walked into the kitchen, adjusting her pink satin robe. "You want something to eat, baby? It won't take but a minute," she said as she smoothed down her wild hair.

"I sure could eat, Mama," Willie responded, patting his empty stomach.

His mother shuffled over to the stove. "It's good to see you, baby, I missed you last week. Now you tell me, eggs and toast or grits with honey?"

"Both, Mama. Been too long since I had your good cooking." He was about to tell his mother how good it was to see her too, but just then Big Jim walked out of her bedroom buttoning up his white, once-starched shirt.

"You 'bout to leave?" Rita called out.

"Yeah," Big Jim answered. "I'll be back sometime. When we can be *alone*."

Big Jim finished buttoning up his shirt without so much as glancing at Willie. Then he opened the front door and slammed it shut on his way out.

"See you later," Rita whispered in her sweet voice. But of course Big Jim didn't hear her; he was already gone.

His mother walked toward the kitchen. "Don't mind him none—he's no good in the mornings. She shifted her tone and found her usual happy cadence. "I'll get your grits. I bet you drove out all this way without nothing in your stomach."

Willie didn't respond. He just shook his head, trying to keep the anger from creeping onto his face.

"What you shaking your head for?"

"'Cause, Mama, I don't understand what you see in him." Willie loved his mama, but as a grown man providing for her, he wanted to tell her his truth. Now was as good a time as any. "That man would sell your soul to the devil if it made him a dollar."

Rita was in Willie's face before he even heard the pot drop to the stove—she was that fast. "I know you grown and you think you know something on life," she moved so close that Willie could smell Big Jim on her, "but if you ever speak to me like that again, I'll whoop you like a child."

Willie backed away from his mother. "Mama, I ain't come here to fight. I jus'… why him? Why always him?"

"Why him? 'Cause he leaves me to my own damn self, for one thing. I never wanted no man poking 'round, acting like he my keeper. And it don't hurt to have a few *extras* 'round here, neither," she said, holding up her pink satin robe. "I farm and you work, but it's still not enough to live comfortable."

"Then I'll work harder, Mama. Send you more of my pay," Willie offered earnestly. "Or I'll move back, drive into town every day. Easy enough now that I got my own truck."

Rita shuffled back to the stove. "You'll do no such thing. An' that ain't no way to talk about your own father either."

"Daddy? He ain't no father of mine! What kind of father don't claim his only son, don't speak a word to him when he sitting not ten feet away?"

"An' for all that, he's still your father." Rita turned around to face her son with narrowed eyes. "He got you that job of yours, didn't he? But you know what he tol' me last night? He say you went behind his back and got work on your own. If you wasn't his son, if he ain't spoke on you good to David, you'd be fired by now."

"My side jobs make things better for us. For you and me." Willie pointed to his mother and then himself. "Big Jim ain't thinking about a future for you, and I ain't got no real future working for him. I ain't aiming to live my life one paycheck at a time."

"That's not true!" Rita barked, but her bite was gone. Willie heard the sadness slipping into her words, and he could see the pain in her eyes.

"Look, Mama," Willie reached in his pocket and pulled out his pay for the Roberson's mantle. "This is for you. I'm working for you. You ain't got rely on him for nothing. I'll provide for you now." He held the money out for her to take.

Rita's gaze flickered between her son's face and the money in his hand. Reluctantly she took the wad of bills as she shook her head, defeated. "Can't no colored man have his own business, and I done told you that many times. It's too dangerous." She was stern, but her anger had melted away. Love lit in her eyes and concerned filled her voice. "You ain't gon' make it out there on your own. You needs a steady job. An' it ain't safe for a colored man to get too high up, you know that."

"I can do this, Mama." Willie moved closer and put his arm around her. He needed his mother to understand. "It'll take me some time, but I can do it."

She reached up and placed a hand on his face. "I told Big Jim you'd stop this foolishness. That job of yours depends on it now, he won't testify on you again. And you *will* stop this nonsense, you hear? I love you too much to lose you."

Chapter 12

"Let me at that cologne you got," said James, reaching past his cousin to the bathroom sink.

Willie popped his hand like he was a toddler. "Get back, now," he demanded before he went back to shaping his hair. "I tol' you to bring back everything you need from home. This here is *my* cologne, an' it cost me a pretty penny."

"Be nice, cousin," James replied in an exaggerated, sweet voice. "You never know, I might find me a respectable lady at this party. Your cologne might be the spark that draws her to me."

"Well, then she ain't meant for you. If it's my cologne she likes, she should be comin' after me." Willie picked up the bottle and dabbed his neck for emphasis.

"You know how it is, I had to get my things together right quick," James retorted. "We was barely home twenty-four hours."

Willie handed the bottle over. "First and only time. Keep this in mind when we go shopping. Get your own personal stuff. A man needs to be smelling good when he steps out."

James eagerly took the bottle, splashed some liquid on his clean-shaven neck, then dashed out of the bathroom. "Thanks, cousin," he yelled as he bolted down the hall and into their room. "You made some lucky lady's night."

Willie shook his head and ran the comb through his hair one more time. By the time he made it back to their room, an excited James was standing by the door, bouncing on the balls of his feet as if he'd never been to a birthday party before.

"Come on, Willie, we gon' be late. Let's get ourselves moving!"

"Calm down. Any woman will smell the fresh on you if you acting like that. Smooth it out a little." Willie pushed past his cousin and into their room. He swept the change on his dresser into his hand, then picked up the few folded bills and place them in his pocket. "Alright. We can go now, but only if you wipe that fool grin off your face."

The ride to the Roberson house didn't take long, and the cousins teased each other all the way there, just like when they were kids. When they arrived, Willie attempted to pull up to the Roberson's home, but cars and trucks packed both the driveway and the curb. "Guess we have to park across the way," he mumbled as he maneuvered his truck across the street to an open spot by the end of a neighboring property.

With the truck parked, he opened the door and stepped one foot out onto the sidewalk. But before he could go any further, James seized his arm. "Hold on, something's up," he warned.

"What?" Willie frowned, but when he looked over his shoulder and past his cousin, he understood: a police cruiser was creeping down the street. The officer in the passenger seat was writing in a notepad, taking down license plate numbers. Willie remembered what Mr. Roberson had said about keeping eyes off of his meeting, and he wondered if he and James should go back to Rosa Mae's.

"Cousin," Willie said quickly, "make like you looking for something in the glove box. Best not to let 'em see our faces."

"I sure don't like this," James whispered as he did as he was instructed. The glove compartment was crammed with stuff, it wasn't hard for him to look occupied.

"I don't either," Willie agreed as the cruiser rolled slowly by. He took a deep breath to gather his thoughts. "But Mr. Roberson is good people. We'll keep up, but let's get going to the party anyhow."

With their earlier excitement now forgotten, Willie and James cautiously got out of the truck and walked with a forced ease to the Roberson's front door. They were the forty tensest yards of James' young life.

"Come on in boys," Earl Roberson greeted as he opened the door. "Kind of you to come. You're right on time, but just about everyone else is here already."

When Mr. Roberson's eyes narrowed at something beyond James' shoulder, Willie turned as casually as he could to follow the older man's gaze. A second police cruiser was rolling past the house. "What's going on with that?" asked Willie, trying not to sound too concerned.

"Nothing, don't pay them any mind, son," Mr. Roberson answered as his eyes followed the cruiser. Once it passed the house, he smiled widely, putting Willie at ease. "They can scout us all they want. All we're doing is celebrating my Brenda's birthday, so do come on in and make yourselves at home." As the cousins walked through the door, Earl Roberson lowered his voice and added, "And not even the law can stop progress."

"Earl, what you talking about?" called one of the men from card table inside.

"Oh, nothing." He sucked his teeth. "Just our friends the police doing their civic duty. Nothing new."

"They still watching us?" another man at the table asked. "We ain't doing nothing illegal. We ain't even gambling—we jus' playing for peanuts." The man held up a nut still in its shell with mock innocence. The whole table laughed, breaking the tension.

Mr. Roberson moved to the center of the living room to address all the guests at once. "Everyone, I don't want any of you to worry. We're having a birthday party. The First Amendment applies to our people just as much as anyone else. Peaceful assembly is our right as citizens!"

Most of the men at the table nodded or mumbled their agreement, as did a few of the other guests in the room. The knot in Willie's gut relaxed a bit.

"Now, I'd like to introduce y'all to Willie Taylor and his cousin James," Earl Roberson continued, still addressing the room at large. "Willie here built our new mantelpiece," he added, pointing to the fireplace. "He's just about the best woodworker in town—any of you can be assured of that much if you call on him."

A smile spread across Willie's face as he nearly blushed in embarrassment. "Pleased to meet y'all," he said, waving his hand sheepishly. Mr. Roberson had been true to his word right from the start.

"You boys must be hungry," Mrs. Roberson broke in. "I'll get you some starters. My sister here made some excellent deviled eggs." She turned to a woman standing just behind James. "Tillie, will you come help me in the kitchen?"

Mr. Roberson put his hand on Willie's shoulder. "Come over here, son, let me introduce you to some fine people."

"Thank you, sir," Willie replied softly, still glowing from the praise he'd just received.

"We're all friends here, call me Earl." Now all of us here at this table are business owners. Most here in Washington Park, but a few out over the county line, too."

"I never knew so many colored men owned businesses," James said to no one in particular. Negros owned small shops back home, but then men at the table were clearly experienced businessmen. Most looked like they knew how to play a mean game of poker, too.

Earl continued. "This is Henry Lovejoy, he owns a masonry company." Henry nodded his head toward the cousins. "And this is Howard Wilson, who runs a carpet and upholstery business. Jack Blackmon owns a lawn and garden service, and Clarence Toliver runs a delivery service—he's got three vans now."

One by one, Earl described what each of the remaining men did for a living. Everyone welcomed the cousins warmly as Willie's head began spinning with excitement. A thousand questions flooded his mind. He wanted to know how they each got started, how they kept their businesses going, and most of all, how they stayed out of trouble.

"Beg pardon, I didn't catch that, sir," Willie said as he realized his thoughts were blocking up his ears. "What kind of store do you own?"

Trevor Brown smiled as he repeated himself. "Appliances. I sell and repair refrigerators, washers, dryers, anything electrical."

"Washers and dryers?" James piped up, excitement jumping out of his every word. "We ain't ever had either of those. I did expect colored folks owned machines like that. Back home, all we got is a scrub board an' a clothesline."

Trevor laughed kindly at James' youth. "I tell you what. When you get a place of your own, I'll sell you a fine washer-dryer set—an' at a friendly price, too."

James smiled so hard his cheeks nearly glowed; someday he'd have a washing machine, just like white folks. "Gee, imagine that," he said wistfully.

"Let's get to business," Earl said, taking a seat in one of the folding chairs and motioning for the cousins to sit down. "I invited you all here to talk about boom coming to Montgomery. There's going to be a lot of growth, and that means a demand for services."

"You're not talking business already, Earl?" Tilly asked as she appeared with a plate of appetizers. "Before your new guests have even had one little bite to eat?"

The men all laughed. "Well, she has you there, Earl," Clarence cried as Tilly set down the plates. The cousins expressed their thanks in perfect unison.

"Earl, Janice asked that I tell you she's attending to the other guests. And Brenda should be here soon. Do try to wrap things up by then."

"Yes, ma'am!" Earl replied, making a mock salute. Some of the men did the same. "We'll be done directly, Tillie."

"I have to admit, I am perplexed some, and I do surely admire y'all," Willie said after swallowing a deviled egg. "Only negro business I ever known was business the white man don't want."

"That's how they want you to think, son," Earl replied. "But this boom that's coming, it's a chance for us to get a share of the pie—if we move quick. And we *can* get our slice. Look at what happened in Birmingham just last year."

"That was awful violent, sir," Willie said pensively. "Fire hoses on students even younger than James here. An' Dr. King himself got arrested."

"That is regrettable, son, but progress always comes with a price. We have to fight for opportunity, and we've got the SCLC behind us. I don't know if you've been up to Birmingham of late—it's already changing for the better."

"Amen to that!" cried Trevor as he held up his glass. Several other men toasted him.

"As to our business tonight," Earl continued, "my brother keeps me up to date on the latest happenings downtown, and change is a-coming."

"Your brother?" Henry lifted his thick eyebrow. "Isn't he a janitor?" he asked as he fanned himself with his cards.

"A janitor in *city hall*. The best position for picking up information!" Earl cried. "He's practically invisible, but he's been hearing some things." Earl paused for effect, waiting until he had every man's full attention. "For one, they're building one of those new-fangled malls with at least twelve stores. On top of that, they have permits for a huge housing development on the east side of town. This is our city, we should get some of that work, too."

Jack spoke aloud what most of the men were thinking. "You know as well as I do how this works. They ain't gon' let us walk up an' take their jobs." The group murmured their agreement.

"We get those jobs by getting there first," replied Earl. "My brother can bring a list of the permits... *and* their owners."

Some men nodded their heads, but a few of the men gasped. "Earl, you know right well stealing that list'll put your brother in danger. They'll string him up in the street!" cried Jack.

"I know. He knows. But this is bigger than the two of us. He'll be smart about it. He's going to borrow the list overnight, return it the next morning. Janitors are the first in and last out—no one will suspect a thing."

Some of the men grumbled, some shrugged, and the rest watched and waited for Earl to tell them more. Willie's good sense told him he didn't want anything to do with this, but the excitement in his gut was arguing otherwise.

"And where *is* your brother tonight?" Clarence asked. "Are you sure you can speak for him?"

"I'm sure. He's gone to Selma with his wife to visit her people for the weekend, but he and I are in agreement. We know the plan's not without risk, but waiting for handouts has been keeping our people's pockets empty." Emphasizing his point, he pulled his own pockets inside-out, "They're making money from our people, but not giving anything back in return. We're the leaders of this city's negro industry, it's up to us to stand up for our own!"

Everyone at the table, Willie included, nodded in agreement. Earl was pleased. He needed unanimous support if they were going to make a real impact for their community and families.

Jack was the first to vocally agree with Earl's idea, "When do you expect we'll have that list?"

"A day or two hence. Depending on how easy my brother can get in there. And then we'll meet again to strategize. Jack, can we use your house for that?"

Jack hung his head. "As much as I want to, I got me a wife and children at home. Plenty of eyes on us already—jus' last month someone threw a brick through my window, mind."

"They know each and every one of our cars," Howard added. "I can't have them trying to hurt my family, either. First Amendment or no, I can't host a meeting, not with the new baby and all."

Ideas bounced across the table as the men voiced their opinions and considered their options. Every man wanted change, but nowhere was safe enough for a meeting.

"We can't always meet here," Earl explained. "We got cover tonight, but too many meetings will only draw attention."

"That's true." Trevor nodded in agreement. He picked up a peanut and started shelling it anxiously. All at once, the men started buzzing with conversation again.

After a minute, Willie shouted over the excitement. "Gentlemen," The table grew quiet as the men turned their expectant faces to their newest recruit. Willie cleared his throat. "I do believe I have a solution." He looked at James, who nodded in knowing agreement. A palpable curiosity filled the air.

"Brown's Boarding House and Café. I'm sure my landlady will host us for just a small fee. Miss Rosa Mae Brown ain't scared of nothing, not even the white man."

Chapter 13

"Daddy, are you still talking business?" Brenda called from the front door. Several guests, including her Aunt Tilly, gave her quick pecks on the cheek as she entered the front room.

"My girl! Earl jumped up and ran to his daughter. "Happy birthday, sweetie." He hugged her warmly, then popped a kiss on her cheek. "We've just finished, I promise."

"I'll believe that when I see it, Daddy," she teased. "But I'm here now and this is my party. I want you to celebrate *with* me tonight."

"I celebrate everything you do, baby. Come step over here with me, there's some young people I'd like you to meet." Earl placed a hand on his daughter's back guided her toward the sofa.

James nearly choked on his pop when he saw Brenda. He'd seen pretty girls before, but Brenda's beauty very nearly made him forget he had a tongue.

"Gentlemen, this is my daughter, Brenda." Earl smiled the smile of a proud father.

Both cousins stood up from the sofa. Willie's face transformed into a sly, yet polite, smile. "Evening, miss." He shook Brenda's had with a long-perfected mixture of strength and gentleness. "A pleasure to make your acquaintance."

With much less finesse, James blurted out, "Hi, Miss Rober... son." Brenda wasn't just a pretty girl, she was a city girl, a college girl. When he looked into her honey-brown eyes, his stomach tied up in knots just like his tongue.

"Brenda here just finished her first year at Tuskegee. She's studying music. My baby's been singing like Marian Anderson since she was two years old."

"I do hope I get to hear that gift soon," Willie stated smoothly. His eyes caressed Brenda's face as she blushed.

"I couldn't have asked for a better daughter," Earl continued. "She goes to school all week and still comes home most weekends to share her talent with our church. Vocals *and* piano"

"I'm sorry I couldn't come home yesterday, Daddy," said Brenda. "Summer semesters sure are intense, and I have my midterm jury coming up this week."

"It's alright, baby, you're here now." Earl replied, before turning to address the room "Can I have everyone's attention, please? It's time to celebrate my sweet girl here. She's twenty years old today."

Claps and whistles filled the room along with shouts of "Happy Birthday."

"Those folks at Tuskegee didn't know they were getting a star, and her mama and I couldn't be more proud."

"Yeah, and she play good too," Jack yelled from the card table. Laughter filled the room.

"You're right about that, Jack." Earl beamed at his daughter. "Sweetie, get on these keys and bless everyone with a song."

"But… Daddy, please." Brenda smiled shyly and shook her head. She really didn't want to perform at her own birthday party. She'd been hoping someone else from the church choir might perform for her tonight instead.

"Come on, now," Janice encouraged from across the room. "Do one of those beautiful spirituals for us."

"I'd much rather if you play for me, Mama," she replied, now blushing outright.

The room exploded. "Naw!" "No way!" Come on!" the guests shouted. Brenda's musical skills had been the pride of the community for years; everyone was looking forward to hearing her sing.

She looked over at her father, whose eyes were glowing with pride and anticipation. Relenting, she said, "Okay, Daddy, but none of that old-fashioned stuff tonight," as she walked over to the piano. "Sister Tharpe is calling to me." Brenda took a seat, then turned to the room. "And I'll need y'all to give me that good rhythm," she said before striking the first chord of "Up Above My Head."

To James, Brenda's voice was just as captivating as her face. Despite the upbeat music, she sang with a peace that calmed him to the core. When she hit a high note with perfect clarity and strength, the hairs on the back of his neck rose. The whole room was clapping along with the beat, but James felt she was singing just for her.

Willie too was awed. He'd never seen anyone perform with more spirit and energy in his life, and watching Brenda's body sway with the music stirred something in him that he'd never quite felt before. He longed to be able to command the piano the way she did. Half of him wished he could caress Brenda's soft skin, the other half wished he could caress the piano's keys and create such beautiful music.

Applause and cheers spread across the room as Brenda stood, took a bow, and then smiled at her father. "Outstanding," Earl pronounced proudly.

"Now everyone, the food's all set out in the kitchen," Janice announced. "Perhaps Brenda will grace with another song later, but for now please do help yourselves to a plate."

The rest of the evening flew by. Earl celebrated with his daughter almost all night, although he did steal away to the card table once or twice. But each time, when Brenda or Janice shot him a disproving look, he'd excuse himself and return to his other guests.

Before long, most of the older guests had gone, leaving only a few of Brenda's cousins along with Willie and James. Janice put Rufus Thomas' *Walking the Dog* on the stereo before retreating into the kitchen. Young people always did need a bit of space.

Brenda began tidying the room as she listened to her cousins' chattering. James saw his chance: "I'll get that for you, birthday girl," he offered as he picked up an empty pop can.

"Oh, thank you... um..."

"James." He smiled and picked up a shot glass. "I'm awful glad to have met you tonight."

"You likewise," Brenda replied. Her response was polite, but intentionally brief. She moved forward, collecting the abandoned napkins and plates.

"You like Tuskegee?" James asked as he scurried behind her. "I'm a senior in high school this coming year, an' I'm trying to gets there."

Brenda frowned. Young colored men who didn't speak English properly grated on her; she had no qualms about correcting misuse. As her daddy had taught, the negro condition would never improve without a basic understanding of correct English.

"You mean you're 'trying to get accepted to Tuskegee.'" She spoke slowly to drive her point home.

"Oh, yeah. That's what I meant." James dismissed the correction and doubled his step to keep up with Brenda. "An' when I do get into Tuskegee, perhaps you'll allow me to take you out."

"Take me out?" Brenda nearly tripped over her own feet. It wasn't that she was stuck up, but James' face hadn't even fully lost its little-boy look. Asking her out took courage, she noted that much, but James was much too young in body and mind for her to accept a date.

James shrugged his shoulders. "A little dinner wouldn't hurt too bad," he said lightly.

"Perhaps we'll talk about it after you're graduated next year," she replied gently. She didn't want to hurt his feelings too badly.

"I'll look forward to that day, miss," James said, trying not to admit defeat. He was sure the thought of Brenda's lips could keep him warm for years.

Earl had pulled Willie into the kitchen to give him some business pointers, but now he passed by his cousin on his way into the front room. Willie appreciated Earl's advice, but thoughts of Brenda had kept crowding his mind. His head spun with curiosity: What made her sing like that? Why did she still come home on the weekends? Did she have a beau? He'd been attracted to plenty of girls, but Brenda *intrigued* him. He wanted to sit her down and study her like a course in school.

"Excuse me," Willie said as he walked over to Brenda and relieved her of the full trash bag she was holding. "Please let me take this outside for you."

Brenda batted her long lashes against her cheeks and smiled. "Thank you, that's awful kind." She'd done plenty of looking at Willie throughout the evening and—after seeing her parents' beautiful new mantle—she wanted to know more about his craft.

"If you'll kindly tell me what you need, I'll be glad to take care of it," he replied, holding her gaze in his as he spoke. "Show me where to bring this, an' I expect we can finish up in no time."

Neither one of them rushed the walk out to the yard. Willie liked being near Brenda; from the slowness of her pace and soft expression in her eyes, he figured Brenda liked being near him, too.

"Your daddy tells me you've been playing piano all your life," Willie said as they walked outside.

"Daddy does exaggerate some," Brenda replied modestly. "Although I did start lessons as soon as I was old enough to reach the keys. Mama always says I have a natural ear for the piano in particular."

Imagining a six-year-old Brenda sitting at the piano bench, Willie laughed warmly. "I've always wanted to learn to play some. Perhaps you'd be kind enough to teach me the basics?" He deposited the trash bag into the metal can, then added, "Not that I'll ever play like you, ma'am."

She took his hand into hers and examined at his fingers. "You have good hands, fine working hands," she offered as she traced the tips of her nails over Willie's calloused palm. She measured the span of his fingers with hers. "And you have a fine reach." She released his hand slowly, then turned to head back to the house.

It took a few seconds for Willie to answer: the flow of blood to his brain had slowed a good bit. "Big hands like my granddaddy's. I expect I could reach a scale high-to-low," he chuckled.

"Why do you want to play?" Brenda asked suddenly, curious about Willie's motives. Plenty of boys had come up with all sorts of reasons to get her attention, but asking for music lessons was a first. Why would a carpenter want to play piano?

"My mama didn't quite have funds enough for a piano, but I always did like the sound of it. Our church had a fine one, an' it was the best part of going to services." He paused for a moment, not sure he wanted to confess the next part. "When I was a coming up, the choir leader let me try a few chords once. He said drowning cats made a prettier sound."

Brenda laughed harder than she intended to. "It's alright," she said sweetly, "I think I can help." Willie noticed the dimple on her right cheek; he stuffed his hand deep into his pocket to keep from caressing it.

"I can pay you some," he offered. "I have a steady day job, and I do aim to have my own shop before too long."

"My dream is to be a professional singer," Brenda explained as the stepped onto the porch. She paused, leaning on the railing. "It's what I've been working for since I was little. And I *will* make it happen."

"Of course you will," Willie encouraged. More shyly he added, "But do you think you can find an hour or two a week to teach me? I never told anyone before, but I really would like to learn."

Brenda looked straight into Willie's eyes, where she found both eagerness and honestly. "I tell you what. We're usually home from Sunday services by one o'clock. If you can come then, I'll start teaching you. No charge, but you have to be dedicated to learning."

"Yes, ma'am, I am." Willie's smile was also his promise.

"Do you have a piano to practice on?"

"My landlord has one at her café. I expect I can use it in the evenings."

"Good, because you'll need to practice every day." She walked into the house with Willie close behind her. "I'll give you your first songbook right now."

He shut the door and watched Brenda stride over to the piano. He somehow successfully kept his mouth from hitting the floor when she bent over and rummaged through the piano bench.

"Go home and practice," she directed as she handed him a beginner's book. "Study your hand placement and keys. Your first quiz will be on Sunday."

"Thank you, ma'am," Willie smiled as he flipped through the book. "But it's only right that I give you something in return. What if I take you to the movies after my lesson? Would you like that?"

Brenda smiled widely, causing the dimple in her check to appear again. "Willie Taylor, I do believe I would like that very much."

Chapter 14

Rosa Mae shoved the cash register shut. She wished

she could shut her ears as well. "Quit making all that racket,"

she hollered over Willie's playing. He'd been pecking at the

keys for what seemed like the last hour, and she now had a

headache.

When he struck another shaky chord, he also struck

Rosa Mae's last nerve at the same time. "Willie!" she

marched over to the upright piano in the corner. "That's

enough now, hear?"

"But you did say I could use it," Willie protested.

"An' Cayson let us go early today on account of the rain.

Can't a man use his extra time to improve himself?"

In reply, Rosa Mae slammed the fallboard shut.

Willie darted his fingers back just in time to save himself

from amputation. "You running away all my customers with

that noise!" she snapped. "I tol' you after-hours, and it ain't after-hours yet."

"But there ain't nobody here, an' I need all the practice I can get," he protested. Learning piano was a good bit more complicated than he'd expected. "I'm starting lessons on Sunday and she say I need to practice first."

"She?" She who?" Rosa Mae folded her arms across her chest; she knew she didn't have any claim on Willie, but that didn't stop a prick of jealousy from rising within.

Willie lifted the fallboard so he could try again, but Rosa Mae slammed it back down. "Come on, don't be like that," he said, caressing the side of her arm and trying to sway her. "Let me practice."

Rosa Mae shook her head and leaned in close to Willie. "Seems like whoever *she* is got your head in them clouds." She rubbed her fingers against her temples. "I guess I just need to see who this woman is before you get yourself into a heap of trouble."

A jolt shot through him, alarmed at the thought of Rosa Mae in full battle mode meeting his kind and refined Brenda. Willie wasn't afraid of much, but the fear he felt told him just how much he liked Brenda.

Rosa Mae turned to walk away, but he tugged at her wrist. "Wait, now," he insisted. He didn't like having to explain himself, but he knew that keeping his landlady calm and happy would be better for him in the end. "I always wanted to learn, an' I finally found someone to teach me, is all."

She turned around and promptly folded her arms. "You ain't never looked at that ol' piano before this week. Damn thing is barely in tune." Rosa Mae had bought he piano secondhand years ago, when she'd intended to keep the café open late on Friday and Saturday nights for private parties. After a few trial runs, though, the thought of spending every weekend babysitting a bunch of inebriated fools put her off the idea. "Who's this teacher you got?"

"Brenda, Earl Roberson's daughter," Willie

explained. "You know, the college girl." His eyes flashed

with excitement; Rosa Mae didn't miss it.

She lifted an eyebrow. "A whole heap of trouble," she

repeated, more to herself than to Willie.

Willie shifted his tone. Now that she'd calmed some,

he sensed a little charm might go a long way. "You the only

person I know who's got a piano, and I sure do appreciate

you lettin' me use it."

Rosa Mae responded in exactly the way Willie had

both expected and dreaded. "Instead of banging on that

thing," she inched her hips closer to Willie and whispered the

rest of her words in his ear, "I know something else you

could be banging on that would sound a whole lot better."

She slid a finger down the side of his neck and brushed her

breast against him.

Willie cleared his throat as he stood up quickly.

Hiding his disdain, he forced a smile on his face and

countered, "Aw, come on, you know I got that meeting. The fellows should be here at the top of the hour. Not twenty minutes hence."

Willie watched as the sultry glow of bedroom thoughts drained from his Rosa Mae's eyes. "Yeah, them new friends of yours," she said, rolling her neck. "I don't know how I let you talk me into this. Now I got to keep this place open an extra half-hour. Plus, I don't need no trouble around here."

"There won't be no problems, we a small enough group. An' anyhow, when do you ever close this place on time?" He walked over to the counter. "Anyone who's interested will think we jus' having our dinner."

"I ain't scared of no prying eyes," Rosa Mae scoffed. "I just don't want this place getting a reputation an' running off my good-paying customers. Don't mess up my money. Don't mess with the men who bring me my money."

Willie could recite Rosa Mae's two commandments by heart. Reassuring her, he replied, "There gon' be a number of men here, an' all of them got money. It'll work out just fine, plus you'll get your feel. I promise you that much, you'll see."

§

The metal bell above the café's door jangled. Conversations continued from outside as the six men entered, shaking the light rain from the coats. Rosa Mae rushed out from the kitchen looking a bit like a pit bull on alert.

"Good evening, Miss Rosa Mae," Earl greeted as he removed his damp hat and placed it on the counter. "I want to be the first to thank you for hosting us this evening. And please do be assured that the only folks who know about this meeting are in this room. I didn't even give my own brother the details."

She grunted in Earl's direction, picked up a towel, and began wiping the counter. The less she knew about the meeting, the better.

"I know you'd normally be closed up by now, so we won't hold you long," Earl explained. "Thank you again."

"You ain't got to thank me." Rosa Mae threw the towel into a bucket in the corner. "You can thank Willie. He talked me into this mess." She walked away without another word, then clicked the deadbolt on the café's door into place.

"She'll be alright," Willie laughed. "That's just her way of saying hello and welcome."

"If that's her hello, I'd hate to see her turn someone away." Earl paused, panning the room. "Where's your cousin tonight?"

"Next door. Gone to bed early. Said he's feeling poorly, though he looked jus' fine to me," replied Willie. "But I don't mind saying, part of me is glad of it. I do wonder if James is a mite too green for what we're discussing tonight."

Earl clapped his hand on Willie's shoulder. "He is very young, that's true enough. I expect he'll come around in his own time—and we'll be glad to welcome him when he does."

"That's mighty kind of you, sir, thank you." He couldn't blame his cousin for ducking out. To James, his job was a way to save money for the upcoming year, but to every other working man, laboring was a way of earning enough to get through the next week. James wouldn't know the difference for some time yet.

Earl turned to the group of men standing behind him. "Gentlemen, start getting settled so we can begin. Willie, please go tell Rosa Mae that we'll each take a plate of whatever she's prepared tonight. Seven orders altogether."

Sounds of murmuring excitement, shuffling feet, and scuffling chairs filled the air as the men pushed three small tables together, then took their seats. They chatted among themselves until Rosa Mae and Willie brought out plates of chicken and greens.

The food smelled good, but none of the men seemed particularly interested in his dinner. Everyone sat forward with his eyes trained on Earl, waiting on him to deliver the news from his brother. Jack, usually the comedian of the group, didn't crack even one single joke.

"The information I have in my hands right now will change our lives forever." Earl began as he removed a large manila envelope from his satchel. He opened it, then held the folder of information up in triumph. "The news is good, gentlemen. There's indeed plenty of development planned for our city." Smiles and head nods rippled around the table as Earl started passing around the paperwork. "Be careful with those reports, gentlemen, mind those collards. I need to get these back to my brother tonight."

"Earl, this one says Cayson got the mall project," Clarence said with disappointment as he read through the folder. "That's no use to us. We'll never get a foothold with them."

"Yeah, they only use colored folks for labors," Willie added. "I should know."

"True," replied Earl, "but the good news—I think Howard is holding the report now—is that Cayson was outbid for the housing developments in on the east side of town."

"Yep, that's what it says here," agreed Howard as he carefully handed the folder across the table to Clarence. "Some other outfit in Atlanta got the permits. Livingston Enterprises."

"And that's where we'll make our money!" cried Earl. "The Hillview subdivision will have two-hundred and fifty new homes."

183

"That sure is a lot of houses, but how we gon' get a piece of that?" Trevor asked. He hesitated before adding, "An' I don't rightly see how construction is any good for my business, anyhow. Automatic dishwashers don't build houses."

"Think bigger!" cried Willie, truly excited by the news. "In a development like this, refrigerators, washers, all sorts of machines come with each home. Someone needs to supply all that."

"Our newest member has himself a point!" Jack exclaimed with a laugh in his voice. "Even beyond the development, there's plenty of dough out there for us *all*. Who you think is gon' do the landscaping for all them shiny new homes? Blackmon Lawn & Garden, if I have anythin' to say on it!" He slapped his hand down on the table as he spoke, prompting cheers and laughs from everyone.

"Trevor's question is a fine one," Earl said over the men's laughter, "and the news is good there, too. I succeeded in reaching Livingston Enterprises just before the close of business today. I talked to the foreman, a Mr. Singleton." The men leaned in, eagerly awaiting Earl's next words. "All the bids he's received from Georgia companies are far too expensive, and he'll be happy to entertain bids from local contractors. Henry, Willie, that's you. He needs as many bricklayers and framers as he can get!"

"And I'll be glad to meet that need," Henry said, nodding his head in agreement. Willie didn't need to speak— he practically gleamed with enthusiasm. Cries of, "The contract's yours," and "Outbid 'em all," rose from the table.

"Just remember… you're not asking for work," continued Earl. "You're bidding as a businessman, and that bid includes the pay for your own manpower. Bidding as a business means getting business-level pay."

"No problem," Henry said with the thumbs up. "I'll stand firm on my bid."

Earl looked over at Willie, "Son, do you know how to place a bid? If not, we can certainly help you."

"Yes, sir, I do. Learned as soon as I started working on my own. Once I see the plans, I can send a bid in."

"Good. Because the way this Mr. Singleton is talking, y'all will need to get started as soon as you can. And mind, none of this is going to be easy. Especially with our head start, the white man won't be happy—there *will* be a backlash. We need to be ready for that."

"They mad at us already, and we ain't even got the contracts yet," Jack interjected. "Henry'll have plenty of material to build with—them white folks gon' be shitting bricks soon enough."

The table erupted as the men laughed away their uneasiness. Willie laughed too. What seemed radical just a few days ago now felt more like a natural progression. Colored folks had just as much right to earn a living at a fair wage as anyone else. Why shouldn't he be a part of that?

"Thank you for coming tonight, gentlemen," Earl said. "I do believe that concludes our business for this evening. Take a few moments to finish up your dinners, but let's not dawdle. I'm going to go have a word with our hostess."

Willie stood up and joined Earl as he walked over to the door of the kitchen. Willie poked his head inside, calling for Rosa Mae. She appeared almost instantly, throwing a dishrag over her shoulder as she walked out.

"Miss Rosa Mae," Earl began, "thank you again for opening your fine establishment tonight. Let me settle up our bill." He pulled out his wallet. "Seven dinners, this should cover it exactly."

"I'll make your change," she replied, walking behind the counter to the register. "Willie's plate is included in his rent." Rosa Mae had bent many a rule over the years, but she never once cheated a customer, and she didn't intend to start now.

"Then perhaps you can add the extra to this instead," Earl said warmly as she opened the till. He pulled an envelope from the pocket of his suit jacket and presented it with a slight flourish. "Your fee, ma'am. Plus, the fellows and I added a little extra for you. Even Willie contributed."

"That's right, I did," Willie added; it felt good to be a part of a group. "Not as much the others, but I did put in some."

Rosa Mae grabbed the envelope and peeked in, running her thumb over the bills inside. Her fee was there, plus a solid ten percent. She smiled in spite of herself. "If y'all gon' pay like this, you can have all the damn meetings you want right here."

Without warning, golden rays of evening sunlight suddenly streamed in through the café window. The three laughed together easily as if Jim Crow could never touch them again.

Chapter 15

Brenda's smile was wide and inviting as she opened the front door, and so dazzling that Willie nearly forgot why he'd come to the Roberson home. The sweat suddenly forming on his brow had nothing to do with the humidity of the hot afternoon.

"You're right on time," Brenda greeted. "I do appreciate your punctuality."

Willie had to force his mouth to form words. He removed his hat slowly, then returned the greeting. "Good afternoon, Miss Brenda." Hardly able to breathe, he reminded himself aloud why he'd come. "I've been practicing just like you said, ma'am." He held up his songbook up as if it were evidence.

Brenda's eyes twinkled. "Glad to hear it. Come on, let's get started." She placed one hand on his shoulder and ushered him toward the piano.

Willie walked slowing, taking the extra seconds to enjoy the warmth of Brenda's touch. "I sure do hope I've done alright this past week," he said earnestly as he walked across the room. He turned and smiled. "I put in practice time near every evening this week—much to my landlady's disliking. I do believe she'll boot me out if I don't improve soon."

At Brenda's sweet laugh, the butterflies in Willie's stomach fluttered that much harder. "Don't worry about that, you're new at this," she replied brightly as Willie seated himself on the piano bench. She took a step forward. "Now, show me what you've been practicing so far."

He took a deep breath, placed his right thumb over middle *C* key, then set his unsure fingers over the adjacent keys. He took another breath before beginning the scale. His notes sounded a bit weak, but he managed the ascending scale without error. Feeling more confident, he then mirrored the scale using his left hand.

"You're doing so well, Willie. Placement is step two."

"Step two?" Surprised and disappointed, he looked up at Brenda. "Did I skip something?" He honestly couldn't imagine what could be simpler than a scale.

She giggled a little before she gracefully placed the length of her hand against the center of his back. "You have to sit up straight," she said, pushing Willie's spine forward gently. The hairs on the back of his neck stood on end at her touch; he prayed Brenda didn't notice. "The first step," she continued, "is always to position yourself with a flat back and square shoulders."

"I'll remember that, thank you." When Brenda smoothed her hands across his shoulders, Willie had to fight back a groan, hiding it with a slight cough.

"Now play what you see on page two." She took a short step to the side to get a better view of her new pupil's hands as he played. Willie pushed away Brenda's fresh, soapy scent and tried to focus on the notes and numbers printed in the songbook. He played the first measure without a mistake, but then fumbled over the next notes as if he'd hadn't spent even one moment practicing.

"That's alright," Brenda encouraged. "We have to teach your hands how to behave. It's all new movements, new coordination. Even if your brain knows which notes you want to play, that doesn't mean your fingers do, too."

"That's a mite like turning a table leg," Willie replied slowly, trying to relate her advice to something he knew. "When you're first starting out, that is."

"How's that now?" Brenda couldn't imagine why woodworking and piano playing were similar, but she did want to hear him out. Over the years, her own teachers had offered many comparisons to help her better understand music.

"Well, it's like this, I reckon. You can have the finest piece of oak in the spinner—that's this piano here. An' you can have the finest teacher in the world—like you. But until you learn how to hold your tools proper and how much pressure to apply, you're always gon' come out with something that looks about as rough as I sound."

"An excellent analogy, Willie! I never would've thought of that, myself." He struck the keys suddenly as she spoke, giving off an awful, atonal sound. Brenda's dimple reappeared as she giggled.

"But let's stay focused," she said as she straightened her face. When she bent down to extend her graceful fingers across his, Brenda's breast brushed up against Willie's shoulder. He prayed that his respectable teacher didn't look down at his lap; his manhood was stirring without his permission. The notes, the keys, and the entire piano had lost all importance. The prospect of focusing on anything other than her softness truly seemed impossible, yet he forced his fingers to move along with hers.

As quickly as she'd had placed her hands atop his, Brenda stepped back a considerable amount to let him play on his own. Watching his efforts carefully, she continued giving instructions for the rest of the lesson.

After his hands had gained a touch more confidence, Brenda said, "I'm so proud of you! I do believe we're ready for your first duet."

Willie wasn't sure he'd heard his teacher correctly. He hadn't even been playing for a full hour yet; a duet sounded much too advanced for him.

Seeing the look on his face, Brenda reassured him. "Don't worry. We're just going to do an exercise. Kids' stuff. Now go back and find middle C. Play the chord for me, twice."

Willie did as he was told, though he wondered what Brenda was up to. A mischievous gleam in her eye had appeared.

"Good, now go up half an octave and do the same," she instructed. Again, Willie did as he was told. "Excellent. I'm going to sing, and you're going to respond with the chord, moving up one scale each time."

"Like in church. But I'm responding in notes," answered Willie. "I'll do my best, surely."

Brenda cleared her throat as he carefully positioned his hands. With all the sweetness he'd ever heard, she sang out, "Moon Don't Go," in the key of *C*. Even singing such a simple line, her voice was so beautiful that again the hairs on the back of Willie's neck again stood up.

Three times Brenda sang out the line, three times Willie responded. On the fourth pass, Brenda's high note was so perfectly stunning that Willie couldn't help but laugh in pure joy as he struck the chord. He wanted to keep the sound of Brenda's pure, enveloping note with him forever.

"I do love those high notes of yours," he said as the last of chord faded away. "Never heard anything exactly like it in my life. Like a guardian angel."

"You're very kind," Brenda said with modest giggle. "But look, you've completed both your first lesson and your first duet. Congratulations!"

"That sure is something for one afternoon," Willie replied, proud of himself but trying to hide his disappointment at the lesson's end. "Thank you. I can't tell you how good making music come out of this piano feels."

"I can only imagine, with you wanting to play for so long." She sat down on the sofa, curling her legs underneath her. "I expect my parents to be home in just about fifteen minutes. Will you stay and say hello?"

"I would like to, yes, but I do believe you and I need to get going."

Brenda raised an eyebrow as she sat up straight. "Get going? Going to where?"

"To the movies, of course. Just as I promised, remember? One lesson for one film. An' there's a three-thirty showing at the movie house. Last show of the day, with this being Sunday."

"I… I wasn't expecting. I… didn't know they showed pictures on Sundays," she stammered. Brenda had never been shy about dating, but the truth was she'd forgotten all about the movie, and Wille had caught her off guard.

The innocent blush that spread across her checks sent a hopeful warmth flowing through Willie. He silently vowed to make her blush like that as often as he could. "Yes, ma'am. Started last year. Noon to five on Sundays. I picked out a show I thought you'd take a liking to. Bought us our tickets already and everything."

"Well in that case, I can't say no, now can I?" Brenda said with a smile. "Although I really should be studying this afternoon."

Willie got up from the piano bench. He walked over to the sofa, lifted her face gently with his finger, and caught her gaze in his. "I'll have you home early enough." He held out his arm like a gentleman. "Come with me."

§

"Did you like the film?" Willie asked as they stepped out into the afternoon heat. He'd picked a mystery with lots of twists and turns, hoping that the complex plot would appeal to Brenda's bright mind. Truth told, he'd spent the last two hours peeking at her facial expressions from the side of his eyes rather than watching the film. He'd stopped himself more than once from asking her what she was thinking.

"It was thoughtful of you, but that really wasn't my type of movie," she relied, crinkling her nose and shrugging her shoulders.

"What do you mean?" Willie frowned.

"I like romantic movies, myself," Brenda explained, although in her heart she knew she'd watch any film if it meant she could sit next to Willie. "Simple and fun. I study all week, just like you go to work. I guess, at the end of the day, I want to see two people come together. There's enough ugly in this world, I don't need to see it in my pictures, too."

"Well, you do have a point there," Willie replied as they strolled through the town square. "I jus' figured you were more of the dramatic type."

Disdain rippled through Brenda. "What do you mean 'dramatic?'" she asked sharply. Why did men always think they could label her?

Willie stopped short. "Beg pardon," he said, tipping his hat. "I just thought who-done-it movies would appeal to you, with you being in college and all. I expected you'd enjoy figuring out the ending."

Brenda narrowed her eyes and scanned his expression. One of the gifts she'd inherited from her father was the ability to judge someone's character. Looking into Willie's green-brown eyes, she felt a pang in her chest; her own shortness of breath told her of his sincerity.

She gave him a soft, forgiving smile. "I'm sure you'll remember, next time."

Willie's heart nearly leaped out of his chest at the thought of a "next time," but he tried not to let on as he smiled in reply. "Let's go sit over on that hill," he suggested, changing the subject and pointing to the small knoll on the edge of the square. "I do have something I'd like very much to speak to you on." He'd shifted his tone, too; his words were serious, but excited.

Brenda didn't reply immediately. She couldn't imagine what Willie now had to tell her that was so important, especially since they'd spent the whole afternoon together. But after a moment, she answered, "Okay, although I do have to be getting home soon. I need to study, and I have to drive back to campus with the dawn."

Feelings bounced around inside of Willie like crickets in the summer as they walked to the intersection. At the light, preparing to cross the street, he took Brenda's soft hand in his almost instinctively. She didn't pull away, which somehow made him both calmer and more excited at the same time.

As she felt his hand encase hers, Brenda silently reminded herself that she was a good Christian woman on a first date. She pushed the thought of his muscled arms and strong shoulders away as they crossed to the knoll.

"Well, it's like this," Willie began as he helped Brenda lower herself onto the grass. "I expect your Daddy told you some about our meeting this week." He paused as he sat himself next to her, keeping a short but respectable distance between them.

"Yes, he said they're building a lot of new homes in the east part of town. He didn't tell me much more than that, other to say you were awful excited."

"That's just it. Thanks to your daddy, I have the chance to bid on the project as a sub-contractor. Not as a laborer, but as my own man with my own crew."

"That's wonderful, Willie!" Without thinking, Brenda shot forward and kissed him on the cheek. But in the next instant she pulled away, realizing her mistake and blushing. She mumbled in embarrassment, but Willie was too stunned to make out her words. He knew she would be happy for him, but he'd never expected a kiss—not even a peck on the cheek.

Brenda looked into the distance, pretending to be preoccupied with something far down the road. But when, after a moment, Willie reached over and took her hand, she again allowed it.

"Thank you, I'm mighty excited too," he offered, trying to save Brenda from her own modesty. Truth was, the spot where her soft lips had touch him now felt as if were glowing, but he refocused his thought and continued. "First thing tomorrow, even before work, I'm gon' sign some papers at city hall. An' as soon as that's done, I can submit my bid—I've got the plans all worked out already." His voice was soft, but firm and serious.

At last Brenda turned and faced Willie again. "It's your dream coming true. And so much sooner than you imagined!" She clapped her hands together in delight. "But why do you sound so... so... hesitant? We both know you can do the work."

He exhaled as Brenda's faith in him washed over him; the rush gave him all the more confidence. "It's not the work itself that I want to talk to you on. The thing is... well... I know we haven't known each other more than a week yet, but I do feel like no one understands what I'm aiming to do the way you do. Like you're my good luck walking."

Brenda lowered her eyes. "Luck is just a small part of it. It's your talent, your work ethic, that'll make you successful… with or without me." She picked at the grass anxiously as she spoke.

He reached over and gently turned her face to his, soaking up the depths of her honey eyes. "But a touch of luck never hurts either. That's why I'm naming my business after you. I decided this afternoon, when you were singing."

Brenda's head felt fuzzy, as if Willie had suddenly started speaking another language. A strange chill ran through her, a feeling that was at once hot and cold. "What are you saying? I don't… I don't know that I follow. It's your company, Willie—Taylor is a fine name for any business."

Willie inched closer just a bit closer, then placed each of his hands on Brenda's shoulders. "Naw," he began, "it has to be after you. I know it sure as the sun rises. Knew it the minute you hit that note." She opened her mouth to object again, but Willie moved one finger to her lips before tenderly brushing his thumb across her cheek. "Tomorrow, I'm registering High Note Construction."

Chapter 16

The waggling tongues of Montgomery were doing their duty. Quiet words were passed around on church lawns, in store aisles, at bus stops. "A negro carpenter gon' build them homes," they said. "Young man's making somethin' of himself," they whispered.

Everywhere he went, the colored men of Montgomery tipped their hats as Willie passed by. Their wives smiled at him in admiration or murmured and pointed from across the street, and a few had even stopped him to show off pictures of their eligible daughters. In Washington Park, Willie was no longer just Willie; he was now "Mr. Taylor."

Livingston Enterprises was so eager to start the build that they'd accepted Willie's bid inside of a week. By the next week, Willie had his crew and most of his materials together. The week after that, Mr. Singleton had driven in from Atlanta to break ground on the site. With the land now being leveled, Willie was set to begin framing the first houses one week from Monday.

A knock pounded at the cousins' door. Willie and James, still in their beds, bolted upright as Rosa Mae burst into their room. Both cousins grabbed their sheets and covered themselves as they shouted in confusion.

"White folks making me come all the way up here," Rosa Mae growled, "before I even got the griddle good an' hot!"

In all the years Willie had been boarding with Rosa Mae, she'd never once burst into his room—unless someone was late with the rent, she left her boarders to their own devices. She roamed through the hallways now and again, but the only time she ever entered the rooms was when she changed the linens on Tuesdays.

"It's too early for this nonsense," Willie grumbled. "Why you up here?"

"Yeah," James whined, pointing at the alarm clock. "We ain't got to be up for a half-hour yet. What you got 'gainst letting us sleep?" He yanked his sheet all the way over his head and rolled over.

"This ain't no vacation for me, neither," Rosa Mae spat. "That boss of yours jus' called, hollerin' like a fool. I said you wasn't up yet, but he wants you in the office in an hour. Both of you."

"David called? This early?" Willie asked, truly alarmed. "Not his secretary?"

"No, not his secretary," Rosa Mae shot back scathingly. "You don't think I know a man's voice? Now get your beautiful behinds up and git. I got my own work to attend." Before Willie could so much as say one more word, she slammed the door behind her and began stomping down the hall.

Willie rubbed his face with his hands, trying to shake off his groggy confusion and take in Rosa Mae's orders all at once. Dread swirled in his stomach like curdled milk.

"Friday or not, we supposed to be on site today, not in the office," James said as he slid one heavy foot out of bed. "I don't know what this is, I know it's no good."

"Surely not good," Willie replied. "No good ever came from a white man's call this early. I can guess why he wants to see me, but you, too?"

"I've never known David to act like this," James added. "He's always so patient. I can't think of one time he's so much as raised his voice at me."

"Cousin, I think you 'bout to learn a few things about this world. Now get dressed. Ain't no use in putting this off."

The pair washed and dressed as quickly as they could. They scrambled downstairs and out the door. As they left, Rosa Mae shouted from the café steps. "Tell that boss of yours I ain't a message service!"

Ten minutes later, as Willie pulled into Cayson's parking lot, the morning's light rain suddenly gave way to a heavy summer downpour. James, with too-little sleep and nothing in his stomach, almost didn't think the day could get any worse.

Constance was waiting for the pair in the hallway, an anxious look on her face. She skipped over good mornings and polite greetings. "He wants you in the back," she muttered almost contritely. "I'll tell him you're here."

Willie nodded, his gut churning even harder now. The last time he could remember being so anxious was when he'd broke one of his grandfather's tools from carelessness. He'd expected a whooping that day, but Papa Abe had only sat him down and explained the true preciousness of tools. Today, however, Willie knew there would be no kindness in store for him.

He led his cousin down the hall to the close, stuffy waiting room for colored men. Most days, any overflow of labors waited in the outhouse, hoping for a job assignment. But on other days, it was the most dreaded room at Cayson Construction.

"We're done for, sure thing," Willie whispered as they entered the unkempt room. "Be brave." He paned the space. Five other men, sitting rickety chairs, waited to be called for even half a day's work. With the rain, there was a good chance that at least one or two of Cayson's regular workers would call out for the day.

"Boys, I need the room," David boomed, stepping through the doorway. "Go wait on the loading dock if you want to stay dry. James, that means you, too. I need Willie alone."

The other men scurried out of the room, but James' feet were anchored to the floor from disbelief, "You want me out on the dock, too?"

"That's what I said," David replied sternly. "Someone will fetch you directly." James looked into the eyes of his friend. The anger he found there was like nothing he'd seen in David before.

"It's alright cousin, go," Willie assured him softly. "I can take care of myself." His words were brave, but he knew trouble had finally found him. Exactly how much trouble remained to be seen, but trouble had come nonetheless.

David shoved the door shut behind James. He spun around, anger gleaming in his eyes. "You really are something, Willie. Did you think I wouldn't find out? Going behind my back!"

"No, sir, I intended to speak to you on Monday, see what we could arrange."

"Arrange?! Arrange?!" David stammered in frustration, as if the word itself were an insult. "There's no arrangement, boy, you're *done* at Cayson."

"I been a good worker these five years," Willie countered. "No one can frame a house quicker. An' we've known each other for years."

"And I expected you'd know better. Building tables and porches for your own was one thing. Big Jim spoke on you, had me look the other way. But that contract wasn't for you, and you damn well know it! High yellow or no, it wasn't yours to get!"

Rage erupted through Willie at the mention of his skin. Before he could stop himself, he shouted, "That contract *was* for me 'cause I'm the one who got it! We got just as much right to work as you do."

"Out!" David screamed. "You're fired, we're done. If you so much as step one toe on a Cayson site, I'll have you arrested!"

"An' what does Big Jim have to say on that?" Willie shouted. "He's my blood, not yours!"

"He may be your blood, but he's *my* father!" David yelled, as if Willie were trying to claim a right that wasn't his. "And Big Jim wants to know where you got the money for the bond. We're sure it's from our coffers—we just can't prove it… yet."

Willie's gut clenched together in a knot of pain and frustration. His own father, his own kin, thought he was a thief. As if he hadn't spent the last five years building himself up by the sweat of his own brow.

Willie took a long, deep, stabilizing breath. "I don't steal," he said firmly, with an icy conviction. A statement so indisputably true that even David didn't dare question it, although he still demanded an explanation. He stared down his employee down until Willie added, "There ain't no bond on that job. Livingston is a Georgia company, an' in Georgia they don't make negros pay extra jus' for the right to work!"

David continued staring at Willie with hellfire burning in his eyes, but he kept the vicious things brewing in his mind to himself. Willie, equally silent, stared right back: he knew there was no use in trying to change a white man's mind, but that didn't mean he would leave Cayson Construction without his dignity.

"On your way out," David finally said, breaking the intense silence. "Tell your cousin to get in here. I need to speak to him, too."

"Ain't no need," Willie, replied, confused. "I can tell him that we can't come back."

"Did I say we were letting him go?!" David's words tore off his tongue so sharply that spit flew from his mouth. "You don't worry about him—I'll give him your last paycheck and have one of my men drive him home later. You just get out of here, and don't come back!"

§

The sun was just beginning it's slow, later-summer descent in the sky, yet Willie was still sanding away at the door of his truck. No matter how hard he scraped and scrubbed, the black, drippy, scrawling, spray paint wouldn't fade completely. He'd driven out to the east side after lunch to check on Livingston's progress; he hadn't been on site for more than thirty minutes, but by the time he'd come back, someone had painted NIGGER on the side of his truck. He'd driven back to Rosa Mae's with an old sackcloth draped out the window to cover it, but no amount of fabric could cover his humiliation.

With what little money he had in his pocket, he'd bought a can of turpentine and a steel-wire brush at the five and dime. A great big circle of sanded-off paint now marred the side of his door, yet somehow the evil word was still faintly visible.

"Looks to me like you've got yourself some new advertising, cousin," James said as he walked up behind Willie, trying to keep things light. He bent down and examined the half-stripped door. "Not a slogan I would've picked."

In no mood for jokes, Willie growled, "James Taylor, either make yourself useful or make yourself scarce!" He flung a rag into the bucket of soapy water beside him.

"Okay, okay, I get it," James replied, a hint of an apology in his voice. He walked to the back of the truck, grabbed a fresh piece of sandpaper, then knelt down beside his cousin. "Between the two of us, we can get the rest of this off, sure enough," he said as he started to work.

"This is what I get," Wille moaned, mostly to himself. "Losing my job this morning wasn't enough. They warned me about this."

"Ain't much different from back home," James replied, attempting to be helpful. "You know they been doing this since even before our grandfathers."

"Don't make it right," Willie snarled. "An' how am I gon' get this repainted when I'm out of work for the next week? I don't got money to burn. But I can't be running a company with my truck lookin' like this, neither."

James hesitated, swiping away at the soapy water with a rag. "Don't concern yourself about that none. I'll take care of it. Like a housewarming gift, but for your business."

"No. You got your own needs to see to. Next year is a big one for you, an' I ain't lettin' you miss out on account of me. I'll go home to mama for a week or two, use the rent to pay for the paint. I can drive into town daily 'til I get High Note up and running. I'll speak to Rosa Mae an' have her move you in with another boarder."

"Naw, I reckon I got enough saved up, I expect I can take on rent for a few weeks," James replied with a weakness in his voice that told Willie he wasn't being totally forthright.

He stopped scraping away at the paint and stared at his younger cousin. James sanded even harder, refusing to meet Willie's gaze. After a moment Willie asked sternly, "And… what else?

James leaned back slowly, shifting his weight onto his heels and training his eyes on the sidewalk. "An'… after you left this morning…" He paused, swallowed hard, then mumbled something too softly for any man to hear.

"After I left this morning, what? What they do to you, James? Speak up."

James let out a long breath. "Well… I hate to say… an' I know it ain't right … but after you left, David gave me a raise."

"A raise?!" Willie nearly dropped his brush in shock. "Are you sure you got that right? From where I stood, it looked like you 'bout to get your hours cut."

"It did, surely enough. "But when David called me into the outhouse, he say I'm gon' take your place. They gon' need a steady framer now, and they pulling someone in from Selma to teach me what you ain't. David thinks I'll be 'most as good as you, in time."

"You do have a knack for it, true enough, but that don't sound right to me. Watch yourself, these white folks will have you in hot water before you know it."

"David just lookin' out for me," James answered. "I ain't happy 'bout what he did to you, but by the way he explained it, I don't expect he had a choice. This is his way of making sure it don't hurt our family too much on the whole, I recon."

Willie sighed and tossed his wire brush into the gutter in frustration. "I keep tellin' you, you got to *learn*. If he were really lookin' out for our family—"

"He *is*! He didn't *have* to give me that raise. He didn't *have* to speak to Big Jim on me. You keep telling me the world don't work but one way, but it ain't true."

Willie's slammed his fist against the truck's door. Why couldn't James see what was plain as day to everyone else? "What kind of father fires his own son for doing nothing but getting ahead?" he roared, hitting the door again. "You ever think on that? Did you?! An' he and David accused me of stealing? Did you know they done that?"

James nodded angrily. "I did, an' I tol' David it weren't so! He believed me, let the whole thing drop. True or not, him and Big Jim could make real trouble behind that, an' you know it. But David let it drop! Promised me as much. As a friend."

Willie jumped up and kicked the front tire. "Then you need yourself some new friends! Friends you can trust. Friends with darker skin!"

James sprang to his feet so fast Willie barely saw him move. He grabbed Willie's hand roughly and held it against his own rich brown forearm. "Sometimes color don't matter as much as you think!"

A red flash exploded in Willie's eyes, blinding him in anger, and he heard James cry out in pain. When his vision returned passed, James was half-laying on the sidewalk, two feet back, stunned. "You ain't need to shove me like that! I'm only telling you what is!"

"You don't know nothing about what is and what ain't," Willie screamed. "White man make you eat shit, an' you thank him for it!"

James stood up, trying to regain his dignity. "I'm gon' talk to Rosa Mae right now, get me a new room!" He kicked over the bucket of soapy water, sending it flying across the sidewalk. "Go on home to your mama tomorrow, see if I care. By your account, we shouldn't be mixing races anyhow!"

Chapter 17

"Lord," Willie called out from the hurt deep in his soul. "I know that we ain't ever had a real close relationship, and I know I ain't always done right. Lord, forgive me for all the things in the past that weren't in your way."

He'd just reached a stop sign when the urge to pray struck him like lightning. Willie didn't know how long he'd been praying for, how many cars had gone around him, or if he looked deranged for talking to himself in the middle of the road. He didn't care, either. He needed a miracle.

With his eyes still closed, he took a deep breath and continued. "I thank you for all my many blessings, oh Lord, but now I need you. You know my burdens. If it's your will, guide my footsteps in the right direction. In your holy name, I pray…"

A blaring horn jarred Willie out of his daze. When he opened his eyes, a young man in a brown station wagon was staring at him. "Hey, mister, are you okay?" he called through the open window.

Willie looked at the car full of teenagers and longer for the simpler days of his own youth. He forced a grin on his face and nodded stiffly. "I'm fine, thank you. I'll get to moving directly," he replied as one of the other boys jeered at the driver.

The young man nodded before pulling ahead. The kid in the rear-facing seat stuck his tongue out as the car drove away.

"Maybe this ain't my time, Lord," Willie mumbled as he put his truck in gear. "Maybe I was too quick to jump into industry." He stepped on the gas. "Lord, I need your guidance." Over and over he muttered, half to himself and half to the Lord above, as he drove absentmindedly through the streets.

Worries swirled in his head. He'd calculated just how much money he would need to get High Note up and running, and those calculations included every cent of next week's pay, plus at least one side job. Even worse than that, he now had to go home to his mama—with his suitcases packed and his tail between his legs—and beg to move back in.

While the drive home had often felt much too long, today it wouldn't be long enough: Willie had less than an hour to find the right words to tell his mama about his fight with James and explain how he'd lost his position at Cayson. To lose a job to layoffs was misfortune, but to lose a job for cause was practically a sin—especially after she'd already warned him, especially with Big Jim in her ear. He could already hear his mother's mixture of fury, fear, and disappointment echoing in his head. How he would make things right by her, he honestly didn't know.

Lost in prayer and worry, the streets of Montgomery had passed by in a haze. When the rumble of a muffler disturbed his thoughts, he looked around at the familiar street and realized where he was. The Roberson home was just a few doors down.

"How did I get here?" he questioned aloud, amazed at where he was. He pulled over and parked just beyond the edge of the Roberson's property, trying to figure out what to do next. "This ain't where I'm supposed to be," he thought, shaking his head. "I got to turn around before the Robersons see me."

Willie tried to move fast, but everything around him responded slowly. The clutch faulted when he stepped on the pedal, something that had only ever happened once before. He tried again, but he achieved nothing but ear-splitting grinding. "Lord, what are you trying to tell me?" he wondered out loud.

As if on cue, Brenda opened the front door. She stepped outside, and Willie instantly knew the Lord had guided him to where he needed to be. She caught sight of Willie's as she opened the roadside mailbox. With a smile as bright as the sun and as wide as creation, she jogged up to his truck. "I didn't know you were coming by this afternoon!" she, exclaimed leaning into the cabin through the window. "All I expected were bills today, but I got a surprise instead."

"I didn't expect to be stopping by, either, it's only…" his words trailed off as he looked downward. Since he hadn't planned on seeing his precious Brenda today, he hadn't rehearsed what to say. Suddenly thankful that the remnants of yesterday's graffiti were on the opposite side and out of sight, he cleared his throat. "I'm on my way home to Mama."

Brenda studied as much of Willie's eyes as he allowed. He didn't look like the same ambitious, energetic man who'd learned almost a whole songbook this summer. "What's troubling you?" she asked.

"I have news, an' I'm afraid it ain't the good kind," he said, his head still hung low. "An' I sure hope you won't think less of me for it." He peeked up; the shame in his eyes met Brenda's concerned. "Tell me you won't think less of me for it."

She reached in through the window and put her arm around Willie's shoulder. "You're a good man, Willie Taylor, I know that much. Go on now, tell me. Whatever it is, I can help... I'm sure of it."

He ran his hands over his tense face twice before beginning. "I lost my job yesterday, an' I had a bad row with my cousin on top of it—the kind kin-folk ain't supposed to have. I'm in a heap of a mess now."

"I hate to hear that, Willie," she consoled. James a sweet young man, and I'm glad I got to know him some this summer. I can't imagine you fighting—the two of you are so close."

"An' the worst part is I don't know what to do about the money I'll be missing next week, or about my new contract—I don't think I can fulfill it anymore." Willie winced as he spoke. He hadn't said those words aloud before; each one felt as sharp as glass as it came from his mouth.

"What do you mean?" The space between Brenda's eyebrows creased with concern. "Everybody is talking about you and Livingston. We're so proud of you. *I'm* proud of you. You don't need that job at Cayson anymore—there's no turning back now!"

Willie clenched his hands around the steering wheel. "How can I? I already took every extra cent I had out of the post office. Without next week's pay, I can't cover my expenses for High Note—an' even then it was gon' be real tight. I was reconciled to borrowing a few dollars from Uncle George if it came to it, but now me and James had that fight."

Brenda placed a calming hand over Willie's tensed knuckles. "Wait here a second. I'll be right back." She smiled sympathetically. "Don't go anywhere," she said, then sprinted into the house.

Willie didn't know what Brenda was up to, but she was the last soothing and sweet thing in his life: he'd wait years for her if that's what she asked. But Brenda didn't need years. Almost as soon as she ran into the house, she ran right back out again. Before Willie knew it, she was at the side of his truck once more.

"Come on in for a spell," she offered. "We can talk more inside, figure this thing out. There's always a light somewhere, even in the dark."

Willie spoke cautiously. "Thank you, but I don't expect this is for the proper time for visiting. Not with your daddy looking out for me the way he's done these last months." He hadn't considered what it would mean to disappoint Earl Roberson, but now Willie added the new worry to his ever-increasing list.

She placed her hand on top of his again, "Come on. Please, at least for a minute." Her dimple reappeared as she smiled encouragingly, weakening his resolve. When she ran her finger softly down the side of his face, Willie gave in.

"Just for a minute," he answered hesitantly, hoping that Brenda's brilliant mind was already formulating a way to help. He trusted in the Lord's guidance; He had brought him to her.

Earl was sitting on the sofa sipping a coke as if he knew company was coming by. "Always nice to see you, son," he greeted. Willie tipped his hat politely; his mouth wasn't working quite yet.

Brenda turned quickly, hiding her face from her father's sight. She winked at Willie as she said, "I have to help Mama with lunch in the kitchen." She turned again, nudging Willie forward with her elbow. "Talk to him."

He looked back at Brenda's expectant eyes and silently agreed. If she wanted him to talk to her father, that's what he'd do—even if the shame in his gut was telling him to run and hide.

The two men watched Brenda disappear into the kitchen. "Have a seat, son," Earl finally said. By the tone of his voice, Willie understood that it was not a request. He took a seat in the wingback chair farthest from the sofa and kept his eyes trained on the floor. He tried to speak again, but nothing came out.

"Brenda tells me you lost your job yesterday." His voice was serious, but it was mixed with something else that Willie couldn't quite identify.

"Yes, sir." He nodded his head slowly. He wasn't sure which was worse: saying the words or hearing them. "They let me go, sorry to say."

"Well, it *was* just a matter of time." Earl rubbed at his chin calmly and thoughtfully, without any hint of disappointment or surprise. "You do know that, son, don't you?

"How's that now?!" Willie exclaimed before he could stop himself. He'd expected Earl to say many, many things, but that was not one of them.

"You didn't think they'd keep you on once they caught wind of what you've been up to?" Earl chuckled as if he'd just told an impolite joke. "I'm surprised it took this long, truly."

"I was depending on them keeping me," Willie explained. "Especially with this still being the busy season."

Earl practically hooted with laughter, slapping his knee with his hand. "You thought they were going to do the right thing?" The gleam in his eye reminded Willie of a toddler who knew he was up to no good.

"I ain't done wrong. Why wouldn't they?" He shrugged his shoulders in defeat. "If I wasn't doing my job proper, that would be something. But that's not the case at all, sir. I'll testify on that."

"Maybe your cousin isn't the only one who's still a bit green." Earl let his laugh drift off before he turned serious. "Willie, you're a threat, you must understand that first and foremost. You're the future of colored industry in Montgomery. If your contract is successful—as I'm sure it will be—you could become one of our wealthiest men. And that's scary as hell for Jim Crow."

"But even with all that, I…" Willie chose his words delicately. "I… I've known the Cayson family all my life… An' my mother… does so much for Big Jim back home."

"Just because that man is your father doesn't mean he owes you anything—at least not in his mind. Men like him would die before accepting a colored son."

Earl's words hit Willie's mind like an uppercut to the skull. "How did you—" Dizzy and off-balance, he couldn't get his words out. No one in his entire life had ever talked about his paternity so openly.

Earl laughed again. "Montgomery is smaller than you think. And with the way my daughter dances every time we speak your name, I had to find out who your people were."

Still stunned, Willie's reply fell out of his mouth. "But you still let me court your daughter? How's that, sir?"

The older man smiled kindly. "I don't expect you had any say in your own birth, son, no more than the rest of us. My daughter needs a good Christian man who works hard and treats her like the miracle she is. Anything else is incidental."

Willie relaxed for the first time since Rosa Mae had burst into his room. If nothing else, he now knew where he stood with Earl Roberson—not as a working man, not as a business owner, but as Brenda's suitor.

"Now, son, back to the matter at hand. I *have* been making some inquiries on your behalf for when this happened. I expected you'd be doing the same, but perhaps that was misguided of me. Maybe I neglected to explain it all to you properly."

"I don't know what to say, sir, and I really don't know what to do next," Willie replied honestly. He was grateful for Earl's kindness, but this wasn't at all the way he'd expected the conversation to go; Willie had been in the world fighting on his own for so long that he almost couldn't recognize the help now in front of him.

"Tomorrow after church, I'll take you to meet a friend of mine. He has a small space for rent next to my office. It's not much, but it'll do. If you agree to re-lay the flooring and fix up a few other things, he'll let you use it for a few months. So you won't need to lease that old space above the bowling alley." Earl clapped his hands together loudly. "That's one expense taken care of!"

Willie's stomach leaped into his throat in excitement, causing his legs to leap up from his chair. "I can do that, sir! I can get started tomorrow if he wants me to."

Earl laughed softly at Willie's sudden elation. "And I know a few folks who need some custom work. The Mariners want a new oak front door, and the Johnsons need a new dining set. They've been waiting on you."

"Sir!—I..." Willie scrambled to the sofa with all the eagerness of a child on Christmas morning. He took Earl's hand and shook it enthusiastically. "It means the world to hear this, an' especially coming from you. Thank you!"

Earl stood up, Willie still shaking his hand. "Making a way for each other is why we formed our association to begin with," Early said proudly. "Now Willie, you'd best get a good night's rest tonight, because I do believe you'll be awfully busy until your contract kicks in."

Chapter 18

"This place is a mess," Brenda grumbled as she swept the broken glass into a pile. Willie sat at his desk trying to puzzle together his paperwork; the wind had whipped in through the broken windows overnight and turned his carefully organized invoice-piles into a scattered mess. He'd somehow managed to retrieve each bit of paperwork without slicing his hands open on the shards that littered both the office and the front room.

"I still can't believe they did this!" Willie snapped. He picked up a rock the size of an orange from his desk and tossed it the wastepaper basket; a loud thunk reverberated through the office as the stone hit the metal can. "And on your one day a week here, too. I'm so sorry you had to see this."

"It wasn't your doing," Brenda replied with a sigh of frustration. "And I've told you before, I'm happy to be here when I can. You do need a secretary." She'd lost count of the number of times they'd had a version of this conversation over the last few months. Because Brenda didn't have classes on Fridays this term, she'd been driving home on Thursday nights to help Willie in the office the next day. Willie accepted her support, but he also felt guilty about it; part of him was convinced he was costing Brenda her dreams.

"But you're not a secretary today," Willie answered in frustration. "Today you're hauling and clearing—it jus' ain't right."

"I can't believe how hateful some people are!" Brenda exclaimed as she picked up one of the bricks and held it up for Willie to read. "Look at what they wrote on this one!" There, in bold black letters, were the words, "Die Coon."

"Damn shame," Willie agreed, but his words had less venom than Brenda's. No matter how vile the cause, he loved the way her nose crinkled and nostrils flared when she was upset. When Brenda was mad, her anger seeped into everything she did. She walked over floors as if they had tried to trip her, she shut doors like they'd swung against her, and she even cleaned things like they had attacked her. Right now, she was practically mashing her broom against the floor, which was making her breasts to ungulate back and forth under her blouse. He wanted to hold onto his anger, but it was difficult to stay mad when someone so alluring was by his side.

Unaware of Willie's wanton gaze, Brenda continued. "Last month they set fire to that stack of lumber out back in the alley, and now this. It's only a matter of time before someone gets hurt."

Although Willie didn't mind watching Brenda pout a little, he never wanted her to feel unsafe. He walked across the room, then wrapped his arms around her from behind, enveloping her in his embrace. Clasping her tightly around the waist and locking her body against his, he whispered, "They're jus' trying to scare us. Don't you worry on that."

"I do worry on that, and I worry on you," she replied. Her words were defensive, but she relaxed into his grip as she spoke, allowing herself to feel loved and protected.

"There are better things to fret about," Willie answered as he tenderly took the broom from her hand and leaned it against the wall. "Now let's take ourselves a break from this cleaning. Stop sweeping the floor an' start sweeping those lips across me."

Brenda giggled despite herself. Willie pressed her body even more firmly against his and began softly kissing her neck and shoulders.

She didn't pull away, not for a long moment. At last she gathered her resolve and said, "You've got to stop," although her words came out in soft pants rather than with any conviction. "Someone might come in. I didn't lock the front door."

Cupping her backside, Willie spun Brenda around to face him. "Ten minutes," he negotiated. He pressed his lips to hers as he began sliding his hand up her smooth thigh.

"Slow down," she tittered as she wiggled out of his embrace and then grabbed the broom. "We've been doing too much of that, anyway."

After scooping her into his arms again, Willie whispered into her ear, "No such thing as too much. Not when it comes to you," Holding her breast with one hand, he slid the other down the curve of her hip, under the soft material of her dress, and in between her pulsing folds. Brenda craned her neck upward and hummed a simple note of pleasure.

"See," Willie said, a sly smile on his face as he glided his finger through her increasing wetness. "This ain't too much is it?"

She moaned Willie's name as he squeezed her nipple with his free hand. "We have to be quick," she whispered, barely able to get the words out.

He lifted her as if she were a feather, pressed her body against the wall, and parted her legs urgently so he could nestle himself between them. "Quick," he agreed, entering her. "But I need you now."

Just as Brenda relented body and soul, the sound of the front door snapped her back into reality. He whole body stiffened. "Somebody's here!" she squealed, hopping out of Willie's arms. She ran to the mirror. "Make yourself decent!"

"That's just noise from next door," Willie cooed. "Nothing to worry about."

"No, someone's here," she cried again, smoothing out her dress and patting down her hair.

"Hey, where are y'all?" a familiar voice called from the front room. "I've come to see just how bad it is this time."

Brenda's eyes widened in panic before she began blowing around the room like sawdust in a storm. "It's Daddy! He did say he'd be stopping by today."

"You didn't tell me as much!" Willie darted across the room, grabbed a pile of paperwork, and leaned himself against his desk, trying to look as if his desire for Brenda wasn't still growing by the second.

"We're back here, Daddy," Brenda blustered as she fumbled with the dustpan and brush. "We're trying to get the office back together."

Earl strolled into the back room with narrowed eyes. He shifted his gaze between his daughter and Willie before he panned the entire space. "The after-effects of your unwanted guests," he commented before his eyes returned to his daughter and her flushed cheeks.

"They messed up the place pretty good," Brenda responded, attempting to look frustrated and angry, rather than hot and overheated.

Willie stepped in front of Brenda to shield her from Earl's investigating eyes. "What I don't understand, sir, is why they broke the front *and* back windows out. Nobody can see the back, so what's the point?" Brenda darted over to the broom and began sweeping again, keeping her eyes lowered.

"The point, son, is the same one they've been making since the Emancipation Proclamation. I know replacing those windows will cost a bit, but you're lucky—in a way, anyhow. Back when I was coming up, you'd be just as likely to find yourself swaying from a tree."

Willie shivered at the thought. "My truck, that lumber, these windows," replied Willie. "Every couple of weeks, something else happens. What do you think, sir, should I move?"

"Move your office?" Earl scoffed. "No, that wouldn't do any good. You'd have to keep moving forever."

"Maybe it would be worth it." Willie shrugged. "Maybe we'd all be safer," he said, looking over at Brenda with concern.

Earl shook his head. "You can't let them stop you, son. It's not fair and it's not right, but nothing will change for us if we're not willing to stand up, stand firm. And I would add that you'd never make money, either."

Willie frowned in frustration. "I'm mighty partial to making money, but I'm none too keen on parting with my life for it."

"It's been three full months," Earl said, steering the conversation into a more positive direction. "How many houses have you framed now?"

"Well, last week's numbers are here in this mess somewhere, but I do know we've got two full rows of houses framed up." Willie smiled proudly. "That puts us ahead of schedule by a bit." He looked over at Brenda and smiled.

"Thanks in part to your fine daughter, here. I get my paperwork done in half the time because of her."

Earl whistled. "Ahead of schedule? No wonder you're a target. You must be making money hand over fist—and money, son, is power. That's what they're scared of."

"Daddy, it's 1964," Brenda piped up. "Why are they *still* doing this?!" She mashed the broom against the floor again.

Earl shook his head. "Sweetie, it's like I always tell you, hate is a complicated thing. Progress comes in increments."

"Increments that aren't fast enough," she muttered and stomped her foot in frustration. Her nostrils flared; Willie's desire swelled again.

Earl moved closer to Willie, placed a hand on his shoulder. "I've got to be going. Walk me out, son."

Catching his eye, Willie saw the earnest concern there. "Certainly, sir. And I do appreciate your advice."

Earl looked at his daughter. "Brenda, I'm closing up early next door—I told your mother I'd help her with a few things this afternoon. Don't you stay too late. We'll expect you home for dinner, and I'm sure you have some rehearsing to do."

"Yes, Daddy. I want to catch you and Mama up on my week," Brenda replied obediently. "I'm composing a new piece for one of my classes. I'll play it for you after dinner."

Earl blew his daughter a kiss as he and Willie walked out of the office and into the front room. When they reached the main door, he wrapped a stern arm around Willie and drew him in close.

"What is it, sir?" Willie asked, alarmed. He'd never seen Earl's mouth so tight or his eyebrows knitted together like this before. "Like you said, we have to stand firm."

"We do. But, Willie Taylor, I'm talking to you as a father now. I know you and my daughter are just doing what comes natural to young people." He paused, choosing his next words carefully. "But see that it doesn't go too far. My Brenda has a bright future. Don't you steal that from her."

Willie looked into Earl's eyes, too stunned to reply. This was the first time the older man had ever spoken to him like this. Willie lowered his eyes and mutter something, but his words were unintelligible, even to himself.

"Remember this, son. I love you like kin, but I expect you to do right by my daughter, come what may. Just like I fought to get you your first contract, I can fight to keep you from ever getting another one just the same."

Chapter 19

"Anything else I can do for you, boss-man?" Marcus asked as he pulled on his sweater. There was a chill in the air this evening.

"Naw, so long as those materials-logs are updated, I can take care of the rest. You go on home to that little boy of yours."

"Well now, I can't argue with that," Marcus replied. "I filled out the logs good, every tool and machine accounted for. There's just that one circular saw that gon' need replacing soon. It ain't cutting smooth like it should."

"I do believe 'bout wore it out." Willie chuckled. "I bought it used anyhow. I'll get a new one for you next week." He picked up a clipboard from his desk and made a note.

"Bright and early tomorrow, boss," Marcus said as he did up his buttons.

Willie walked over to his foreman and shook his hand. "Thank you for your good work today. I know you fightin' that cold an' I appreciate all you do." Willie made sure to thank his men every day. Running a business was one thing, running a business *right* was another. He never wanted his employees to feel like they weren't a vital part of High Note, never wanted a single man to feel the way he had at Cayson.

With his hand on the doorknob, Marcus replied, "This morning, my wife promised she'd have a heaping pot of chicken stew ready for dinner tonight. That'll fix me up jus' fine. See you tomorrow, sir."

He sighed contentedly as he locked the door behind his foreman. Running High Note was even more work than he'd thought, but the effort was well worth it. The contract with Livingston didn't just make it possible for him to own his own business; it made it possible for him to offer fair-paying jobs with respectable working conditions to good family men like Marcus.

"Work don't stop because the day do," Willie happily half-sang to himself. "Got to get ready for tomorrow on today." This evening, he needed to put together the supply order to submit tomorrow. He always ordered a week ahead of his needs—it didn't just keep the project running smoothly, but it also meant his men didn't lose a day's pay due to shipping or other delays. So far, the only time his men had been off a day was the morning when he'd found his lumber pile smoldering in the alley.

Concentrating diligently as he sipped his coffee, he drew up his list. "Sixteen-D nails, ten gross..." he muttered as he wrote. "Sandpaper, forty-grit roll..." He kept costs tallied in his head, but he also wrote down the amount for each item neatly in the adjacent column.

A knock at the door startled Willie out of his concentration. It was five-fifteen, and he figured he was the only man left on the block. He grabbed the baseball bat he'd begun keeping under his desk; no telling what kind of trouble could be waiting.

Walking into the front room, Willie peered through the plate-glass front door. There stood James, cap in hand, a pleading look on his face. Willie dropped the bat and broke into a run—he hadn't seen James since their fight, and he imagined that something must be wrong back home.

Throwing open the door, Willie asked breathlessly, "What is it? Is my Mama poorly? Your sisters?"

"Naw," answered James. "Nothing like that. I didn't mean to concern you that account. It's jus'… jus'…"

Willie stiffened, annoyed. "Spit it out. I'm tryin' to close up for the day," he said curtly.

"Amends," muttered James, the word sounding guilty in his mouth. "I come to make amends. We ain't done right by each other. Let me come in, cousin."

"No we ain't, that much is true." Willie stepped back, allowing James to enter. Willie has been working too hard and too many hours to give much thought to reconciling, but the guilt still gnawed at him in the nights. "I jus' don't know what to do 'bout it, though," he added.

"But I miss you, cousin. You're making this whole new way for yourself, an' it weighs on me not being a part of it. An' my birthday… I ain't never had a birthday without you before. Plus, with Thanksgiving coming next month, my Mama will be missing you something awful. Can't we… jus' say a few words, work this thing out?"

"Come on, coffee's in the back, still hot," Willie answered, pointing to the office. "I suppose we still kin."

James panned the office. The space was small, but the flooring and windows were new, and the walls looked recently painted. The filing cabinets and one overstuffed chair appeared used, but the desk looked as if Willie had refurbished it with his own hand.

"I suppose I shouldn't have shoved you like that," Willie began slowly as he poured a mug for James, "but honest... I didn't know I'd done it till I saw you on the ground."

"I deserved it," James conceded. "We practically brothers, an' family should know better than to go 'round salting wounds."

The two men, steaming mugs of coffee in their hands, talked for a good half hour, with each apologizing first, explaining second. It wasn't long before they felt like cousins again, and soon they got to chiding each other just like they'd always done.

"Come on outside for a minute," James said, setting his empty mug down on the desk. "Before we lose the sun completely. I gots something to show you."

"Outside?" asked Willie. "Why didn't you jus' bring it on in with you?" '

James smiled mysteriously. "'Cause I wouldn't want to mess up your fine shop here." He rose from his chair and headed into the front room. "Let's go."

Willie followed, wondering what in the world James was talking about. His little cousin had to be up to something big.

"Over here," James said, pointing to a parked car. He jumped up beside it and threw his arms out with a flourish. "You like my new ride?"

"Is that a Chevy Chevelle?" Willie asked, stunned. "They just started making 'em this year. How'd you get yourself one?"

"I went out and bought it," James answered definitively, full of pride and grinning as if he'd suddenly become a millionaire.

"How's that?" Only a few months ago, his younger cousin had been carrying his clothes around in a shopping bag instead of a suitcase. "You ain't saved up that much this summer. I know what they paid you."

James puffed up his chest proudly. "Not money from this summer—I'm a working man now. With my raise, it didn't make no sense to go back to school, not when there was money to be made."

"What?!" Willie tried his best to keep his anger from rising—he didn't want to start fighting again, not after they'd just made up. "You ain't had but a year of school left. An' what about college? You was set on Tuskegee."

"I was for a spell, but I couldn't go back. I spent all summer with men—honest working men—I couldn't stand a whole 'nother year with a bunch of high school kids. An' anyhow, I'm learning a real skill now that I'm framing. Don't need no diploma for that."

Willie took a deep breath to steady himself. "And what did Uncle George have to say on that?"

"He wasn't happy, true enough, but he don't have much to say now. I got me an apartment over on Singleton. It ain't no palace, but the ladies seem to like it jus' fine. I been aiming to find me a girl equal to your Brenda."

"An' Aunt Thelma? I wouldn't be surprised if she whooped you like you was five."

"Mama don't like it neither, but she say I can take something called a G-E-D exam. Passin' that is 'just as good as gettin' my diploma."

"You'll have to study at night," Willie said. "Wrangling a greased pig is easier than that test. A few of my men took it." He nodded his head as if agreeing with himself, then began walking slowly around the car. He pretended to admire the Chevelle's sleek design, but really he was calculating in his head. Totaling up every cent James made over the summer, plus estimating his pay for the last few months of work, didn't even come close to equaling enough money for a new car and an apartment.

"It is a fine vehicle," Willie conceded as he finished circling the car. "But I can't get the figures to work. What am I missing?"

"A new business, a new girlfriend—you ain't missing much, cousin, except a ride like this baby here," James teased.

"I'm serious now, the numbers just don't add up. What are you up to?"

"Aw, you worry too much," replied James as he began polishing the shiny red hood with his elbow. "I jus' got me a little loan, is all. A boost up in the world jus' to get me started out right."

Willie raised an eyebrow in response, but he didn't reply otherwise; he was afraid he might lose his temper if he spoke too quick. A loan was never a "boost up." Debt was always an anchor—an anchor that much heavier for colored folks.

"Cayson Construction offered me financing," James added, smiling confidently. "They'll jus' take installments out of my check each week till I've paid it back in full."

Willie covered his face with his hands and groaned. He peeked out from between his fingers and said, "You mean to tell me that you let them people talk you into a loan?!"

James took a step back and frowned. "They didn't have to talk me into anything. I jus' told David 'bout my daddy being mad an' wanting me to finish school. David didn't want to lose another framer, so he offered to help me out."

Willie shook his head and balled his fists but kept his voice even. "Helping Cayson to more money is all he doing."

"I only gots to pay a little interest, that's all. David was generous. He gave me a good rate."

"Ain't no such thing as a good rate on interest being paid!" Willie shouted, finally losing his patience. "Paying money to your own employer? How do that make any kind of sense? It's slavery by another name!"

James took a big step back to give Willie some breathing room. "I ain't come here to fight again," James said firmly. "Calm down." He waited until Willie's shoulders relaxed a bit before continuing. "Slavery is one-hundred years passed, cousin, an' this ain't the same by no account. This loan is starting myself off good so I can get myself even better."

Willie wiped his brow and took another deep breath. He gazed at the Chevelle for a long moment, then turned to meet his cousin's eye. Tempering his tone he said, "I wish you'd come to me first. You a jus' about grown now and I can't tell you what to do, but we could've at least gone over it together. How much they taking from your pay? You got enough to live on decent?"

"Well... my check *is* a bit leaner than I calculated," James began, embarrassment creeping over his face, "but I'm

okay, cousin, I am. Truly. My way ain't your way, but…
but… maybe you can try an' be happy for me?"

Willie walked the few steps that separated him from
his younger cousin and threw an arm around him. "James,"
he began, "I'll always be behind you. An' that's why you've
got to come to me first from now on, even if we're rowing.
Blood is blood."

Chapter 20

Brenda's paper-thin hospital gown should've left her with a chill as she waited in the sterile room, but she was hot. Sweating-in-summer hot. Her nerves had taken over—she'd come in this afternoon thinking she would receive her tests results, which would indicate the cause of her symptoms. She'd thought one of the nurses would merely hand her a prescription, but now Brenda couldn't fathom why she needed a second exam so soon. The walls were closing in as she fanned herself with a pamphlet. Every now and again she had to wipe heavy droplets of perspiration from her brow as the long minutes ticked by. What was wrong with her?

Despite her anxiety, Brenda also wanted a nap. She's been exhausted for weeks with no discernable cause. She slept just about every chance she could, and she hadn't even had the energy to drive home last weekend—not even to see Willie on Saturday afternoon. Earlier this week, when she started vomiting and missing classes, she'd decided to come into Tuskegee's clinic. Falling behind in her studies wasn't an option. If that happened, her parents would make her give up her Fridays with Willie at High Note.

After forty-five minutes, Dr. Waller finally appeared. "Good afternoon, Brenda," he said as he sat down on the black rolling stool. "How have you been feeling?"

"Not well," Brenda reported honestly. "I'm still exhausted, and this morning I was so dizzy that I had to sit down for a spell. Yesterday the vomiting got so bad that I just sat in the restroom."

"That sounds about right." Dr. Waller nodded.

Brenda couldn't imagine what was right about taking up residency in a bathroom. The only time she'd even thrown up like this was when she'd had the measles as a child. What could be so very wrong with her now?

Dr. Waller leaned forward and put his hand on Brenda's forehead. "What's this sweating?" he asked. "When did this start?"

"The nurse said I had a low-grade fever, sir, but mostly I think it's just nerves. I can't be sickly. There are three weeks left in the semester yet, and I need to finish it with high marks. My parents saved up my whole life to get me here."

The doctor smiled softly. "I don't think finishing the semester will be an issue, but you might have some challenges coming in the new year."

Her stomach dropped into her feet. She gagged, feeling as if she was about to vomit again. Dr. Waller grabbed the trash can with one hand as he steadied her back with the other. She didn't vomit, but her dry-heaves lasted nearly a full minute.

"There now, I didn't intend on frightening you," the doctor said kindly. "But we have your test results back, and I do have news." Brenda looked straight at him, her eyes wide as saucers, pleading. "At first I thought you had that flu that's been going around campus," he continued, "but that's not it. In fact, there's nothing wrong with you at all. Brenda, you're pregnant."

Choking on her own saliva, Brenda coughed in an attempt to save her life. She gasped as the exam table seemed to shift beneath her. She grabbed onto its vinyl sides with all the strength she had left.

"That can't be right! We... took precautions." She hesitated, struggling for the right words. "Willie always... he always... *removes* himself," she whispered. Every time. We've been very strict about it."

"Withdrawal is not effective," Dr. Waller replied almost sternly. "And some say that's interfering with nature. Abstinence is the only reliable and legal way to prevent pregnancy."

"Pregnant? Pregnant?" Brenda repeated the word, hoping that it would change. Inside of two minutes, she'd gone from fearing for her health to fearing the future itself.

"According to the test…" the doctor began, but Brenda wasn't listening. The word *pregnant* pinged around in her ears, adding to her dizziness. All of a sudden, *pregnant* was the most terrifying word in the English language. Her entire future seemed to shatter before her.

"I'm in school," Brenda cried to no one in particular. "I've got goals." She lay back on the exam table, putting her hand over her eyes. Doctor, how could this be?"

"Diagnostic pregnancy tests are still new," he explained, "and they can return false positives. We can run the test again, but in your case, I do believe the results are accurate. Especially with your symptoms."

Brenda's tears suddenly unleashed in a deluge of racking sobs. She lay muttering to herself as heavy tears ran down her cheeks and neck and soaked the top of her gown.

"Mama… what will Mama… and *Daddy*! Oh no!" What would become of her now?

Dr. Waller handed Brenda a box of tissues without a word. He placed a reassuring hand on her shoulder and waited a few moments until her sobbing lessened a bit. Then he said gently, "Brenda, I do need to examine you. Scoot up a bit for me."

It took a moment for the instructions to register as she watched Dr. Waller pull on a pair of rubber gloves. She looked around the room as if she suddenly didn't know where she was. She sat up half-way, took a tissue and blew her nose, then finally answered, "Yes, sir," as she repositioned herself.

The doctor's fingers felt cold they pressed and searched—first against her stomach, then in the places where only Willie had ever touched. Brenda felt as if his hands were seeking out a tumor or blockage, not the new life forming she was apparently now carrying. She was suddenly relieved that

Dr. Waller's skin matched hers; having a white man examine so intimately her would've been mortifying.

He finished examining her and confirmed the test. "Yes, eight weeks along, or thereabout. When was your last monthly?"

"Some time ago, sir, but that's not unusual for me. My mama says lots of girls aren't as regular as you might expect." She broke into a fresh round of sobs. "And I had no idea."

"We can keep an eye on you here for a month or two, but soon you're going to need a midwife to oversee your care. If your family doesn't have one, there's a clinic in Montgomery for colored women." He lowered his voice and added, "They've seen many young woman in your situation."

Brenda's head reeled again. The phrase *in your situation* reverberated in her head. How had this happened, when all the experienced girls in her dorm had promised she was being safe? She hugged her arms around her own body, fighting back more sobs and trying to keep the room from spinning.

"Listen to me, young lady. This is not the end of the world for you," Dr. Waller said as he helped her sit back up. "You're going to have to make some big decisions, but do remember you're not alone. Your beau will do right by you if he's any sort of man."

That's when it hit her. A chill crept up her spine, practically paralyzing her. She hadn't just ruined her own future, but Willie's too. She tried to respond, but the shock overtook her as the exam table seemed to reel again. The room faded away as the blackness overtook her.

§

Brenda moved her left foot up and over the concrete step, and then did the same with her right. She'd given herself a full week to consider what to do, and although she'd come to a decision, she feared she lacked the resolve to go through with it. Having missed two consecutive weekends at home, she knew she had to act now, before anyone suspected. She walked up another step, bringing herself that much closer to what she knew she now needed to do.

The thought of being a mother made her chest hurt, but the thought of telling anyone about the baby made her want to lie down and stop breathing altogether. Confessing her sins to her parents—who had put so much trust in her and who had sacrificed so much—would end her world as she knew it. Telling Willie that their love had brought hardship would sentence her to a living hell. She'd considered going deep into Lowndes County, to the woman there who could make female problems disappear, but the risks were too great, and in her soul she knew taking a life to redeem her own was no redemption at all.

The only option, she'd decided, was an immediate transfer to Howard University in Washington D.C., where she could study in the School of Music for a year. She didn't know how she would keep up with her classes, but at least in D.C. she could have the baby quietly and give it away to a good family. She'd filled out the transfer paperwork yesterday, and she planned to tell everyone that she'd been offered a slot at Howard because of her exceptional grades. A feasible enough plan; except for one *B* her very first semester, she'd made straight *A*s during her time at Tuskegee.

But she couldn't face Willie, not even if she mustered all her strength. She'd come to Brown's Boarding House today with a Dear John letter and a heart broken into ten thousand pieces. She had no doubt in her mind that Willie loved her, but she couldn't—wouldn't—be his obligation. A marriage of necessity was a marriage filled with resentment; that was no way to make a life together.

Brenda climbed the last step. "Colored Working MEN only," the faded sign in the window read like an omen.

Before she realized what she was doing, found herself flying down the steps, feeling as if she were fleeing for her life itself. "I can't do this!" she cried aloud to the setting sun.

She ran a good twenty feet before her better sense got ahold of her. Breaking Willie's heart would be the hardest thing she'd ever done, yet it would only be worse for him if she disappeared without an explanation—even if that explanation was a lie. Willie had a brighter future ahead of him than all the other boys she knew combined; Brenda couldn't take that away, no matter the circumstance. He'd be hurt, no doubt, but he'd find another girl; these days there was no shortage of Montgomery women vying for Willie's affections.

Collecting herself, she decided it would be easier to go into the café instead. She smoothed her dress, took several long deep breaths, then scurried to the screen door as if she were tearing off a band-aid. She burst into the café breathlessly, where Rosa Mae was behind the register making change for a customer.

"Oh no. You turn yourself right back around," Rosa Mae ordered as she handed the man his change. "You know damn well I only allow working men in here."

Brenda bristled as the customer walked passed her and out the door. The last thing she needed was a fight with Rosa Mae, but she couldn't let this cannonball of a woman scare her off, either.

"Beg pardon, ma'am," she began carefully. "I'm not here for supper, and I'll let you be just as soon as I can. I only wanted to leave something for Willie." Brenda flipped a neatly folded envelope out from the pocket of her dress. "Can you make sure he gets this note, please?"

The request stopped Rosa Mae in her tracks, her damp dishrag falling to her side and her eyebrows folding together. She planted a hand on her hip before asking, "How come you can't give that to him your own self? Y'all together like peaches and preserves every weekend."

"I know, but things... have changed." The hurt seeped into Brenda's words as she fought back pressing tears—she knew better than to show any weakness to Rosa Mae Brown. Yet she didn't have a plan B, and if Rosa Mae wouldn't help, she didn't know what she would do. "Please!" she cried, holding out the letter as if it were a life preserver.

"You best be glad I got my furniture moved last night." Rosa Mae pursed her lips and flattened her upturned palm against the air. "Give it here."

Accidentally letting a tear of sorrow and relief escape her eye, Brenda stepped forward to place the envelope into Rosa Mae's hand. But before she could release it, Rosa Mae snatched her hand away and plunked it right back on her hip.

"Wait, what you got tears for?" she asked as she lifted her perfectly arched eyebrow in suspicion. "You trying to break things off with Willie?"

"I... Well... Because..." Brenda fumbled through the words as her eyes searched the walls for relief from Rosa Mae's suspicious gaze. "That's... between me and him," she finally managed.

"Naw, not me." She shook her head as she strolled back along the counter. "You ain't about to turn me into the witch that done Willie wrong. I ain't equipped to handle no grieving man."

"Miss Rosa Mae, please just—"

"—Sorry little sweetie," she replied as she swiped her hand and the dishtowel dangling from it across the air. "Whatever news you trying to escape, you need to give it to Willie on your lonesome."

In response, Brenda burst into tears, her words incoherent. She leaned against the counter for support, feeling as though she might faint again. She slowly lowered herself onto one of the stools, defeated and helpless.

Rosa Mae softened a bit as she watched the young woman before her crumble. She tilted her head and grimaced. "Sweet child, that man loves you like a bee love pollen. Things in his world wouldn't work right if you wasn't a part of it. I can't have no hand in ending that. An' Willie's one of the few honest-to-God good men who come through these doors. Don't make me hurt him on account of you."

"I don't know if it's like that," Brenda replied. "Not now, anyhow." She let her eyes fall to the scrubbed-clean counter. "I have to get back home," she continued. She fished around in her pocket and pulled out a crumpled bill. "Here, you can have this too, for your fee. But please, I need you to take this to him."

"Take what?" came a man's voice as the screen door banged shut.

Brenda froze. The buckshot curls at the nape of her neck nearly straightened themselves out and stood on end.

Frantically, she balled up the envelope and dropped it to the floor, kicking it under the counter with her foot.

"Willie, you mighty early this evening," Rosa Mae said, trying to distract him while giving Brenda an instant to wipe her eyes. "I'll go fix you a plate. Roast beef and mashed potatoes tonight. That roast should be done and ready by now." She sauntered into the kitchen and out of sight.

Longing and panic tussled in Brenda's chest in equal parts. No one could help her now: she'd have to face Willie with this lie. A lie for his own protection.

"What are you doing here?" Willie asked as he walked over to Brenda and pecked her on the cheek. "A welcome surprise to be sure, but how is it my landlady hasn't thrown you out?" he chuckled.

"Sure enough, I tried," Rosa Mae called from the kitchen. "An' I was about to get her gone, too!"

"I thought you had a recital tonight. I didn't expect you to drive home until the morning," Willie continued as he took Brenda's hand in his and guided her up from the stool. "You oughtn't be missing anything that counts for your grade. Are you alright?" He paused for a moment, searching her face. "You don't look exactly well."

"I'm alright," she began as she forced herself to remove her hand from Willie's. "I just…" She cleared her throat. "I needed to—"

Before Brenda could finish, Willie noticed the discarded envelope on the floor. "What's that?" he asked, reaching down and scooping up the wadded paper.

"That's why I've come." She pointed at the envelope as Willie began cautiously smoothing it out. "I'm here to leave you that note."

Rosa Mae stuck her head out from the kitchen. "Willie, we ain't even close to closed yet, and customers be coming for the dinner rush," she hollered. "Go take that poor child into the storage room before you open whatever that damn thing is." Some mixture of concern and annoyance flashed over her features; more softly she added, "Don't everyone need to hear your business."

Willie's confused glare squeezed at Brenda's heart. She needed to escape. "I have to go, Willie," she said softly. "Just read that and know I'm sorry." She strung her words together so fast that she barely took a breath in between them. She moved her feet almost as fast as she turned and ran, but she didn't flee quickly enough to escape Rosa Mae's bellow.

"Naw, little girl!" she called out, stepping fully out of the kitchen. "Come back here! If you big enough to write it, then you big enough to explain it."

Brenda didn't mean to stop, but her feet betrayed her and anchored her to the floor. Willie had been good to her, earnest and truthful and heartfelt. He'd shared his secrets with her, even the ones he was almost too scared to admit, and she owed him nothing less than the same. Suddenly she wanted nothing more than to keep the man she loved from reading her letter of lies. She whipped herself around and looked Willie straight in the eye.

Willie, more confused than he'd ever been, managed to string together four words, words that were both a command and a request. "Come talk to me."

Steadying herself, she stepped a few paces closer to him. He reached out to take her hand, but Brenda recoiled. "I'll stay, but only if you don't read that," she said with a resolve that surprised even herself. "I'll explain. *Please* let me explain." Willie nodded hesitantly in agreement, tore the envelope in half twice, and then threw the pieces into a trash can.

In the storage room, Willie set out a folding chair for Brenda, then sat himself on an old milk crate. Brenda twisted one hand inside the other, and gnawed on her bottom lip, and darted her eyes across the shelving, looking at the rolls of aluminum foil and boxes of dried foodstuffs. She couldn't pull the words together to explain things honestly, so she waited for him to speak first.

"First thing to say is, I love you," Willie began. "But I don't know what's weighing on you, so I don't know what the second thing to say is."

Keeping her eyes trained on the floor, Brenda didn't answer. She didn't want to cry anymore—she wasn't even sure how her body could produce more tears—but rivers began draining from her eyes once again. She gasped and gurgled, but the words would not come.

"Come on, now," Willie said as he hooked an arm around her waist and pulled her into the warmth of his embrace. "Whatever it is, it can't be as bad as all that," he soothed as Brenda sobbed into his neck. "Remember what you told me? There's always a light, even in the darkness." He placed his palms against her wet cheeks and lifted her chin until he could look her in the eye.

Brenda pulled her face away and again nestled herself back into the crook of his neck: she couldn't find the strength to look him in the eye as she whispered her news.

Surprise tinged through Willie's body, shooting into his toes and fingertips. "Say it again," he insisted as he hugged her even more closely. "Did you say… Do you mean to tell me… you're having a baby?"

"They tell me I'm some two months along already," she cried, her voice quivering. "And I just don't know—"

With more force than he intended, Willie pulled Brenda to her feet and looked her straight in the eye. "I'm going to be a daddy!" he exclaimed joyfully. "Me, with a pup of my own. I can't believe it!" He beamed with excitement as he hugged her ecstatically. "Brenda, my Brenda!" he sang, rocking her back and forth and knocking over a mop in the process.

Feeling the deep rumble of Willie's laughter echo through his chest, Brenda's tears slowed. Of all the scenarios she'd envisioned, joy had never once occurred to her. Relief washed through her; she smiled for the first time in a week.

"I can't believe you're so excited." She sniffled as she wiped the tears from her eyes with the back of her hands. "My world's coming to an end."

Willie softly pressed his lips against Brenda's left cheek, right cheek, forehead, and then lastly her lips before he spoke. "Honey, your world isn't coming to no end, *our* world just beginning."

She folded herself into Willie's arms once again, fear still in her voice. "My daddy is going to kill me. Or he'll kill you, and that would be worse."

"Sit up and listen to me." He clasped her shoulders and guided her away from his body until he could see her face. "On our first date, that first piano lesson, I knew you were my destiny. That's why I named High Note for you."

"You did?" Brenda asked faintly.

"I did. No doubt about it." Without warning, Willie slid down onto one knee, Brenda's hand in his. "You know it's not official until I ask your father, but—"

"No! Wait!" Brenda pulled her hand away from Willie's warmth. "This isn't what I want," she blurted out. She grabbed a napkin and began twisting it between her hands. "That's... why I wasn't going to tell you."

Deep worry lines instantly marred the smoothness of Willie's forehead as disappointment shot through him. He couldn't imagine the rest of his life without Brenda, especially now that she was carrying his child. He mouthed one word, "Why?" but couldn't reply beyond that.

Brenda firmed her mouth and pushed down the tempest of fear, shame, relief, and confusion. "I need to finish school, come hell or high water," she explained. "And you can't marry me, raise this baby, support us, and expand High Note all at the same time." She rubbed her face, then extended a hand to help Willie up. "I can't take that from you, not when you're doing so well. I don't want you marrying me on account of this."

"Brenda Roberson, I have no such intentions," Willie began soberly before his voice suddenly turned light and playful. "Did it ever occur to you to ask why I'm home so early today? When I got a whole crew to run and houses going up left and right? When I got so much paperwork that I have to rely on you 'most every week?"

Brenda blinked in confusion. She'd been too distraught to question why Willie had walked into Rosa Mae's at 4:30 p.m.—if anything, she'd believed it was fate playing games with her.

Willie spoke gently but moved assuredly as he closed any space between them. "Brenda, you're a part of everything I am and everything I dream about. When I look at you, I see my future—an' I don't want my present to be without you, either."

"That's how I feel, too, Willie, but we have goals. We never talked about a baby. We never talked about marriage."

"That's because talking's not the same as doing," Willie replied, fumbling around in his pockets in the dim light. "I went to do some shopping this afternoon," he added as he pulled something from his jacket, his eyes twinkling in excitement. "I was aiming to give this to you at Christmas, but I expect here in this storage room will have to do."

He shot down to one knee again, opening the ring box as he moved. "Brenda JoAnn Roberson, I hope you will do me the honor of becoming my wife."

Chapter 21

"I don't know how you ever got yourself back into Earl Roberson's good graces so quick," Rosa Mae remarked as she sat back in her recliner and heaved her weary feet onto the ottoman. "That man had such *plans* for his girl. Then you come along."

"It did take some doing, I'll say," Willie answered, sipping his tea. "We did have the good sense to show Earl the ring first," he continued, "then tell him 'bout Brenda being in the family way. That might've helped some, right from the start."

Ever since he'd started High Note, he and Rosa Mae occasionally sat together, after the café had closed, in the boarding house's small but cozy sitting room. Rosa Mae had her own tea blend of chamomile and other herbs to help soothe the body after a long day, and Willie was grateful for it. Some days he worked until his back and neck were screaming with knots, and the tea ensured him a good night's sleep without resorting to liquor. With the wedding coming up less than two months, and with so much to do between now and then, Willie needed his sleep now more than ever.

"You always did have smarts enough to use the brains the good Lord gave you," Rosa Mae chuckled. "An' I suppose Brenda could do worse," she said, eyeing him up and down lustfully. More to herself than to Willie, she muttered, "That girl did get a good deal."

"Once Earl seen we have a plan in place, a real way forward, he came 'round. Janice wouldn't have it no other way. She let him stew for a couple weeks, then put an end to it. Said she wasn't 'bout to let the blessing of a grandchild become a curse on her family."

Rosa Mae nodded in agreement. "You only done what jus' about every man and every woman before you done." Her eyes glinted libidinously. "What kind of world would this be if we ain't do what comes natural, baby?"

There was a time when her innuendos would've scared him off, but now he barely noticed them—and since Willie was now engaged, Rosa Mae didn't take exception to her advances being ignored.

"I wasn't expecting him to help us with that land, though. That was mighty kind of him. We wanted to buy a plot quick, and he was amenable so long as Brenda's name was on the deed next to mine. He called it our wedding present. He couldn't have known it, but that's gon' allow me to build our home without taking out any kind of a loan. Debt is no way to start a life together."

"True. Debts do have a way of spreading like brushfires. Every time you think you got one under control, another one pops up." Rosa Mae leaned back in her well-broken-in armchair. "But you sure you gon' have that house done fast enough?" You only jus' got started."

Willie beamed with pride and excitement. "Sure will. We only moving into her parents' place for a spell. I aim to be done an' ready to move in by July, maybe even June. Gon' be a big house too, with a bedroom for our pup an' an extra one for my cousin. One of James' sisters is gon' come live with us in September. She'll be a big help—Brenda gon' start back to school part-time after Labor Day."

"Well don't you got everything wrapped up nice and neat? With a bow on top an' everything," Rosa Mae exclaimed, not even bothering to hide how impressed she was. She'd always known Willie would do good for himself; she'd seen every kind of working man under God's sun, yet Willie stood apart from just about every single one.

"Bet that means you gon' miss me 'round here," Willie chuckled. "I ain't lived nowhere else except my mama's. This place is almost a home."

"This ain't no home to anyone but me," Rosa Mae scoffed, turning back to her usual guarded self. She lifted one foot from the ottoman and began massaging it. "Men come, men go. That's what y'all do—an' that's the way I like it.

Don't make one lick of difference who's here and who ain't, so long as I get my rent on time."

"Don't mess with your money. I know I know," Willie chuckled again as he swallowed the last of his tea. The brew was already working its magic; he could feel the knots in his shoulders slowly unclenching.

"An' don't you think for a minute that I don't got your room rented already," Rosa Mae continued. "A young fellow from Tuscaloosa movin' in the week after you move out. Gon' be a porter on the rail line, an' he needs a place to stay while he trains. Paid me a fee to hold the room for him."

Willie shook his head, laughing to himself. "Of course he did." He stood up from the sofa with his empty cup in hand, then grabbed Rosa Mae's empty mug as well. "Don't mess with your money," he repeated as he walked into the kitchen.

"Which mean you best not get cold feet," she called as Willie walked away. "'Cause you officially kicked out the moment you say 'I do.'"

§

Brenda bounced through the skeleton of the house like she was on a pogo stick, and the baby growing inside her seemed to giggle every jostle. Just being on the site for the first time excited her. Even though her new home with Willie was far from finished, she was grinning from ear to ear.

"I can't believe how fast you got this up," Brenda said, touching a bare beam with glee. "We really are going to have our own place!"

"Yes, baby, for the three of us," Willie rubbed his hand over Brenda's just-starting-to-swell belly. "We've been so blessed. Marcus and the crew have been donating shifts on Saturdays as our wedding gift. I didn't even ask—they insisted. We'll be done sooner than I thought, and under budget, too."

"When you treat people right, it comes back to you tenfold," Brenda said, proud of the way Willie ran his business. "High Note is good to its employees, and they're good to us."

"Paul did the padding and laid down the foundation in less than four days," Willie explained excitedly. "The crew and I framed the house in a little under a week. Henry Lovejoy gon' do the exterior brick—I've seen his masons work, they'll be done in no time."

Brenda laughed at his eagerness. "You'd think you never built a house before."

"I never built a house for *my family* before," Willie answered, swooping behind his fiancée and wrapping her in his arms. "I only wish we could have this ready for our wedding night," he whispered, kissing her neck.

Brenda turned around and kissed him gently on the lips before firmly pushing him away. "None of that, now." She pointed to her stomach. "That's how we got into this situation in the first place," she giggled.

"And I'd do it again!" Willie exclaimed exuberantly.

"Willie Taylor!" she rebuked. Brenda screeched as a wicked, shocked delight shot through her. "Focus. You're supposed to be showing me this house," She skipped across the site and spun herself around one of the beams. "How long till they start drywalling?"

"Some time yet," he answered. "Plumbing's got to go in first—all we got in now is the main under the house." He pointed to the other side of the site. "Gas line, too. After that, we'll get the electricity installed proper. Two or three outlets in each room, real modern-like."

Brenda nodded as she scanned the space dreamily. Willie watched the tempting curve of her backside as she reached down to pick up a blueprint.

"Do you know where we're standing right now?" he asked, eager to hear her guess.

She opened the rolled-up plans and studied the markings for a moment before looking straight into Willie's eyes. "It looks like we're standing… inside a small room off the living room? It's much too big to be a closet, but a mite too small to be a sitting room."

"Hey, I didn't know you could read blueprints!" Willie said proudly. The alacrity of Brenda's mind never ceased to amaze him. "When did you learn to do that?"

"The library at school has just about everything, and I've been reading up. Pretty soon I'll be able to read plans better than you."

"Naw, you should be studying on your music. Leave building to me. We've got to get you graduated before you can become a star."

"True, but we've got to get this house together first," Brenda answered. "And I want to know what this little room is. You've been talking my head off about these plans, but you never once mentioned this room." She walked around the space, examining it thoughtfully as if the walls were already in place. "How come all the other beams are up, but these ones aren't?"

"On account of this room being framed special, interior work only. Materials coming next week," Willie's eyes glowed mischievously—Brenda knew he had a secret and was enjoying teasing her.

"Come on," she said, stepping toward him and running her nail softly down his face, "what are you up to? We'll be married inside of a month, no secrets, now."

"Well, I just got to thinking…" he took the blueprint from her and pretended to study it, building up the suspense. "I mean, it wasn't in the original plans but… I jus' moved a few things around here… an' again here…"

Brenda couldn't stand it anymore. When the baby fluttered in her stomach, as if eagerly awaiting the news too, she snatched the blueprints from Willie. "*What* wasn't in the original plans?"

"Your music room!" Willie burst out with a gleeful laugh.

Brenda's whole body lit up with excitement "My what?!" she exclaimed as the dimple on her cheek appeared along with her smile.

"You still gon' need to practice, even if the baby is sleeping. So I'm making this little room for you. With soundproofing. You can practice all day and night—our little one won't hear a thing."

Brenda practically jumped into Willie's arms as the joy surged through her. "How'd you ever think of that?" she asked. "I sure am marrying the right man," she announced with a sweet laugh.

"An' later on, when our kids are grown, all we need to do is take down the panels to expand the living room," Willie said. "I got the idea in a trade magazine."

"I can't believe… I can't believe you did this for me!" She wrapped her arms around her fiancé's neck, pushing her body against his. "Thank you, truly," she said before kissing him deeply.

Willie gazed into his beloved eyes, relishing it the overjoyed light within. "An' when Willie Jr. is old enough, you'll start him on piano lessons. Sitting right on his mama's lap like a little king."

"Oh, so I'm having a boy, huh? Are you sure on that?" she asked, the corners of her mouth turning up slyly. They hadn't talked about the sex of the baby yet, but there was no doubt in her mind that the child in her womb wasn't a boy.

Willie shook his head. "I just got a feeling," he replied. "I expect you're gon' give me a son. A pup I can teach the trade to, who can take over High Note when we're old and gray."

"Maybe someday I will. But since I'm the one having this baby, my intuition might be a bit keener than yours." She threw her head back and laughed. "Soon it'll be you, me, and little Tonya."

Surprised by her assuredness, Willie asked, "Tonya? Where'd that name come from?"

"My Daddy's sister. I told you about her. She's the one who went on home when I was in high school. I want to name our first girl after her."

Willie smiled tenderly. "Tonya is a right pretty name... an' your Daddy will appreciate it, surely." He reached over and caressed Brenda's stomach again, already overwhelmed by the love he felt for the life inside. "You, me, and Tonya, together under our own roof. For the rest of our lives."

Chapter 22

The bell atop the café door jingled as Willie trudged through. His thick boots clumped against the floor in a slow steady rhythm as he made his way over to a stool at the counter. He was ravenous—he'd spent half the day at Livingston's site, half at his own home—and his entire, weary body was looking forward to some good food. When he saw LeRoy slouching at the counter, Willie almost turned around to head for his room, but his growling stomach vetoed the idea.

"I can't stand that yellow nigger," Le Roy grumbled before Willie even made it past the small square tables. "He always in here."

Rosa Mae, who'd been totaling up the money in her till, stopped mid-count to scowl at LeRoy. "You want to stay on that stool, keep your fool mouth closed. You done nothing but bother my customers all day. Hush up. Don't make me have to tell you again." She wrapped a rubber band around the flat bills and tucked them in her apron. "Or else Sally and I will send your ten-cent coffee-drinking ass out the door."

Willie didn't hear LeRoy's reply, and, for the sake of LeRoy's own safety, it was fortunate that Rosa Mae didn't hear it either.

"Don't worry about him or his ugly mug, Willie." She cocked her head toward LeRoy. "You a paying boarder—at least till your wedding day. An' that means you get supper. Like always."

A toothy smile cracked through Willie's frown at the mention of his nuptials. "Wedding plans coming along real good, just the final touches left now," he offered. "I don't have much to do on that; Brenda and her mama are planning everything."

"Good," she replied, pushing a plate in front of Willie. "Let Brenda plan the wedding she wants. All I need to do is show up."

"That's what I intend on doing," Willie agreed. "Although money getting tight now with the house going up. If I could earn every day from now until the wedding, I would."

"Then you in luck. Sam Carter came by earlier. He say a white man needs his house jacked up—the foundation's giving. You know anything 'bout that kind of work?"

LeRoy spoke up as Willie chewed a heaping mouthful of food. "You could've saved them words, Rosa Mae. Yellow Bone don't know nothing 'bout that. He don't know much, from what I hear."

Irritation pushed Willie up from his stool. "You don't know nothing about what I know, LeRoy," he growled, clenching his fists. "An' I know plenty about honest work. Something you ain't much acquainted with yourself."

Rosa Mae cut her eyes at her chronically underemployed customer. "No one here is asking you to stay. You can move your own self along at any time."

"You know I don't like his yellow ass," Le Roy muttered, the right part of his lower lip curling down and nearly touching the cleft in his chin. "But that kind of work can be dangerous."

Willie ignored LeRoy and looked over at his landlady, "Yeah, I know some about jacking up a house, and Marcus does too. Where's the job?"

"Capitol Hill, over on the other side of town." Rosa Mae strode over to the phone and picked up a slip of paper. "This here's the details. Pays mighty well, too."

Le Roy let his eyes wander over Rosa Mae's curves. "You always ignoring me, when I don't do nothing but spend my days giving you attention!" he whined as he started toward the door. "I'm gone."

"Good," Rosa Mae yelled at his back. "I ain't interested in your attention, I'm interested in your money. Spending a dime with no damn tip—you barely worth my time."

Willie shook his head as the café door slammed shut. "Every other day you tell him to git, but he always come back," he said. "How come you put up with it?"

"I can't control what that man do, an' this here is a place for men. Wouldn't do my reputation no good if I threw a paying man out—even if he don't spend much."

"Business first, huh?" Willie asked, smiling slyly.

"Business first," she agreed. She handed Willie the slip of paper. "An' here's the information for your business. It's too late to call tonight, but you best git to it first thing in the morning. You ain't the only contractor in town, and this ain't even your specialty."

"This is jus' what I need to give us a little breathing room," Willie replied, sheepishness creeping into his voice. "We comin' in under budget on the house, but I didn't calculate exactly right for all the things we need *in* the house. I do believe the Sears and Roebuck catalog is now Brenda's best friend."

Rosa Mae threw back her head and laughed heartily. "Men never do," she uttered in between breaths. "Keeping a place right—that *costs*. Y'all have no idea how much work we do."

Willie's landlady was still laughing wickedly as the café door swung open again. "Rosa Mae, I sure do miss your cooking!" called James, smiling broadly.

"Well look who the cat dragged back on in!" she replied. "But go on an' lock that door behind you—it's after closing time already."

"Cousin!" cried Willie, a delighted smile on his face. He hadn't seen James since New Year's Day, when Uncle George and Aunt Thelma had hosted dinner for the whole family. He shot up from his stool and tackled his younger cousin in a bear hug.

"How you doin', cousin?" James laughed from inside Willie's hug. "I been meaning to catch up on you, but this the first chance I got. When I ain't find you at the office, I figured you gon' be here."

"This family reunion best be quick," Rosa Mae instructed, setting a plate down for James. "Or you can take it next door. Either way, your marching orders be in effect as soon as finish you last mouthful."

"Yes ma'am," James replied with a salute. "Orders received." He lowered his hand and pointed to his plate. "Thank you kindly, I got everything I need right here. You can go on an' close up the kitchen if you want."

"I been meaning to check in on you, too," Willie said as James dug into his dinner. "But I ain't hardly had a minute to myself in weeks. Too much to do already, an' I spend every extra hour I can find crafting furniture for the house. Even my mama is missing me." He turned to the kitchen and called, "Rosa Mae, put my cousin's dinner on my bill for the week."

"I already done that!" she shouted back, her tone full of curtness and aggravation.

The cousins laughed together, long and easy. "No one at Brown's Café eats for free," James said. "Don't mess with her money—I remember well."

The two sat together catching up. James marveled at how different their lives were just a year ago, back when he was in high school and Willie was little more than a laborer at Cayson. It hardly mattered, though; inside of five minutes the pair were thick as thieves once again.

"I do have to admit," James finally said, "that I have another reason for comin' to see you tonight. I'm hoping you can help me out some."

"Good," answered Willie, nodding his head in approval. "I tol' you to call on me with anything."

"You ain't gon' like it…" started James, "but I do have to say you were right. Money's a bit too short with that loan to pay, and Cayson can't give me no extra hours till summer. Can you use me for anything?"

Willie swallowed hard. Truth was, with the costs he was facing, now wasn't a good time to take on an extra man, but at the same time he wouldn't turn his cousin away. "Well, my crew is full up, but..." he started as his mind thought on a solution, "Rosa Mae jus' passed along this here job. I was planning on jus' Marcus an' me, but I do reckon I could use a third man on this one." He pointed to the paper he'd laid on the counter.

"You doing side jobs when you own a business?" James laughed, reading the details on the paper. "You moonlighting for yourself?"

Willie grinned. "Yep, I reckon I am. If you think being single costs, you should try being almost married. But in any case, you can help me with that job for now. After the wedding, I'll try an' find you some hours."

"I knew I could count on you! Even one extra day's work this week would be mighty helpful."

"Probably not this week, I expect it'll be next. I got to buy me some jacks first—we ain't have 'em at High Note. They'll take at least a week to come in, even if I order tomorrow. We'll probably be on site weekend after."

James counted the days in his head. "You mean to tell me you intend on jacking up a house on Saturday, then getting' married on Sunday?"

"If that's what it takes, that's what it takes." Willie shrugged.

"Naw," said James. "I can get you them jacks in a day or two, an' it won't cost you a thing."

Willie's face turned quizzical. "How's that? You started a wholesaler without telling me?" He elbowed James playfully.

"Naw, but we got plenty of jacks at Cayson, more than we need. Half of 'em just sit in storage, doing nothing but gathering dust. David will let me borrow a few, I bet."

"James, sometimes I wonder if you right in the head," Willie replied, surprised but not angry. "Don't you remember how David kicked me out? You lucky you still have *your* job."

James played with his food for a moment, pushing it around his plate as he thought. "That is a point," he conceded. "But… but what if it were *business*? What if I asked to let you *buy* some of them old jacks? What David need extras for, when he could sell 'em an' make himself a profit?"

"Now you're using your head," Willie answered. "Money does talk. An' having them jacks this week would speed things up."

"Good. I'll swing by David's office an' talk to him after my shift tomorrow. See, cousin, when we put our heads together, everything work out jus' fine."

Chapter 23

"Can I have a word with you, David?" James called as he walked through the outer office toward David's private space.

"That's Mr. Cayson to you, boy!" commanded Big Jim as he whipped around in his chair. James was shocked, stopping in mid-stride at the inner office's threshold. It was after-hours already, and Big Jim hardly ever came to the Montgomery office anymore, except on Friday afternoons after the colored employees had been paid.

"Daddy, it's James," David said calmly but firmly. "He has some nerves." Big Jim only grunted in response.

"Beg pardon, Mr. Big Jim, sir." James tipped his hat. "Mighty nice to see you this evening," he added with a forced a smile on his face. Big Jim had tolerated James' friendship with David, but the man had never approved of it, and he took every opportunity to make his feelings known.

"James, you do know this is mighty irregular," David said, cocking his chin ever so slightly at Big Jim, hinting that his friend needed to be more professional than personal. "But I can give you a minute, if you're quick."

"I do, sir, yes, and I thank you in advance for your time," he answered, deferring into the role of an employee. If he wasn't careful, Big Jim would surely kick him out. He couldn't allow for that, not with Willie counting on him.

"Yes, quickly, boy," Big Jim grumbled. "We have things to do."

"Is there a problem on one of our sites?" David asked. "The foreman should report that, not you."

"Naw, sir, nothing in that regard. I jus' finished framing up a house today, in fact. Gon' be a beauty, I expect," James reported before turning to Big Jim. "Although I do want to take this opportunity to thank you for all Cayson's done for me. The raise and the loan, especially."

"My son's feeling is that you deserved it," Big Jim said dismissively, showing his disdain. "He runs this office."

David glanced at his watch. "Come on then, out with it. I do need to get home to Mrs. Cayson." Under his breath he added, "You know how she is about punctuality."

"Well, it's like this…" James began, reciting the words he had practiced all day in his head—words that he hadn't counted on Big Jim hearing. "I was wonderin' if Cayson might be interested in parting with some of them old jacks you got. We can pay, of course."

"Don't you answer that, son." Big Jim lifted his head from his folder, turned around again, and eyed James suspiciously. "Boy, I know you're not making the same mistake as that cousin of yours. If you branch out on your own, I promise you it'll cost you your job—and we'll expect our loan paid in full, too, or I'll have the sheriff after you."

James swallowed his anger, although he didn't quite succeed keeping the smile from drooping from his face. "No, sir, nothing like that. I'm a Cayson man," he managed. He took a deep breath, biding his time. "But I do come on behalf of High Note. My cousin is in need of some equipment, an' he called on me to approach Dav… Mr. Cayson here."

"What's the matter with you, boy?!" Big Jim shouted, reaching behind himself and banging his fist on the desk. "Your cousin already cost us that development… can't he just leave well enough alone?! Haven't we given him enough already?"

"Daddy," David began, jumping in before Big Jim lost the last of his temper while also saving a scared James from having to reply. "We do business with these smaller outfits all the time. Circumstances aside, this is no different."

"Circumstances here *are* different," Big Jim shot back firmly. "And you're one of the few who knows *exactly how different* this circumstance is. I'll hear about this from his mama, too, I'm sure. Damn woman!"

Now that the subject of Willie's mama had come up, James wanted nothing more than to flee. "I ain't meant no wrong in coming you to, Mr. Big Jim, sir," he said, desperately hoping to turn Big Jim's crimson face back to its normal hue. "We can leave it be, though. I didn't aim on vexing you none." He tipped his hat again as he turned to leave.

"Hold up a minute," David called as James took his first steps away. He turned and looked his father in the eye. "Daddy, I know you're none too keen on the idea, but we do have a dozen spare jacks and a contractor willing to buy them. And we do need the storage space."

Big Jim opened his mouth to protest, but David cut him off. "Let's give Willie what he wants—it'll save you a headache the next time you're in Lowndes County. Besides, you always taught me business first."

Big Jim leaned forward are crossed his arms petulantly. "Fine," he announced, spitting out the word like a bullet. He couldn't stand having his own advice thrown back at him—especially not in front of a negro—but he'd address it with his son later, in private.

"I have to give you credit James," David began, "you always are brave enough to go for the middle ground. I've seen in on-site, and I've seen it again here today." James smiled for the first time as David leaned over and began scribbling on a notepad on his desk. "So I'll give you a fair price." He ripped the sheet of paper from the pad and handed it forward. "This is what we want for all twelve, but not a penny less. Paid in cash, in full."

James glanced down at the paper. "That *is* a fair price, thank you. I'll collect the money from my cousin tonight, then pick up them jacks direct after my shift tomorrow, if that would be convenient."

Big Jim grunted, but David ignored him as he answered, "That'll be just fine. I'm in Selma tomorrow, but

I'll have one of my men ready them for you. Give the payment to Constance."

"And close the door behind you!" Big Jim snapped, almost before David had finished speaking. James expressed his thanks again, tipped his hat for the third time in ten minutes, and fled. He was proud of having made the deal for Willie, but mostly he was relieved—he never liked being in Big Jim's sites.

With James gone, the two men returned to their work, going over the month's accounts. It wasn't until a few minutes later when David suddenly asked, "Daddy, when was the last time those jacks were safety-rated?"

"I couldn't tell you," answered Big Jim curtly. "I'm not a foreman. I pay people to do that type of thing." Irritation crept onto his face again. "You know that well."

"I'll check the logs tomorrow, just to be safe. I'll have to dig into our records, for the last year or two, though. Could take some time."

"You'll do *no such thing*!" boomed Big Jim as he jumped up. "I need you with me at that meeting in Selma tomorrow. Draw up the invoice now and mark the sale as-is."

"But Daddy, shouldn't we…"

"—No 'buts' about it. I'm not losing a second contract on account of that nigger!" He kicked over his chair to drive home the point. "And if you want the down payment for that house Mary has her heart set on, you'll *do as you're told*."

David felt himself shrinking under the weight of his father's anger. There was no arguing with Big Jim when he got like this, and David knew there'd be no peace for him if he and Mary didn't move out of their cottage soon. Living on Big Jim's land was little different from living in Big Jim's house; his wife's patience was wearing precariously thin.

"Okay, Daddy," David sighed, relenting. "You win. Do as you say and mark the invoice as-is."

Chapter 24

James pulled up to the site early. He'd hoped to beat his cousin to the job, but he should've known better. Willie and Marcus were already there, unloading their equipment. It wasn't even 7:00 a.m. yet; James began to suspect that his cousin had simply given up sleep altogether.

"Hey, 'bout time you got here," Willie called from across the lot, teasing. He said something to Marcus, then made his way toward his cousin.

"I know, I know—go to start early to finish early," James called back as he stepped out of his car. "I remember."

"What's this here, now?" asked Willie as he slapped the hood of James' car. "What happened to them fancy new wheels of yours?"

"Well… I jus' done what I thought you'd do. I sold all that flash an' got me this Dodge Ledger. It only got two years on it, an' I cut down my debt by near half."

Willie smiled broadly in approval. "You're learning some. That's a fine decision you made for yourself."

"It's 'bout the same shade of red, though, mind. I weren't about to give up *all* my style."

Willie laughed loud hard. "Fair enough. You can have yourself any color car you please, so long as the numbers work right."

"An' speaking of doing sums, did I tell you I'm aiming on my G-E-D? Gon' take me a night prep course at the local high school come summer. I got myself enrolled already an' everything."

"James!" Willie cried out as his eyes gleamed with joy. "I'm proud of you." He clapped his cousin warmly on the shoulder. "Glad to hear it. You building a solid future for yourself now."

James blushed as he shrugged. "Come on, let's get to work. Marcus waiting on us." He moved to start across the lot, but Willie grabbed his arm.

"Hold up, I do have something to speak to you on first."

James looked at his cousin, puzzled and slightly alarmed. He'd never once known Willie to delay a morning's work, not even for a cup of coffee. "Is everything alright?"

"Everything fine. This jus' gon' take but a moment. Brenda and I got to talking…" Willie kicked the dusty curb with his boot as a shyness washed over him. "An' we was thinking, if you're amenable… we'd like for you… to be our baby's godfather."

James somehow smiled at the same moment his brows knit together in surprise. For a split second, he looked like the little boy Willie so fondly remembered. In the next instant, though, James was eighteen again, with his whole future ahead of him. "Godfather? Me? Gee… that's… that's a real honor, but…"

"But nothing. There's no one else we'd rather name. Even more, now since you just shown how responsible you can be."

James shrugged again. "It's jus'… Well, I do try to an' keep myself to the Good Book, but… I guess I don't know much about being a godfather. You know cousin Logan passed on when I still a little thing."

"Yes, I remember," Willie said somberly. "He was a kind man, an' Papa Abe's best friend in this world. Shame you didn't get the chance to know your own godfather better." He reached over and put his arm around James. "But all a godfather needs to be is a decent Christian man. You're both of those. Everything else gon' follow suit."

James chewed his lip pensively for a moment, considering. This was a lifelong commitment, and he'd never thought so far into his future before. "An' you really think I'm up to it?" he finally asked.

Willie nodded firmly. "I do. No doubt in my mind. Brenda knows it, too."

A smile washed over James' face as he held out his palm to shake Willie's hand. "Then I'm proud to accept, cousin. I promise you, I'll always do right by your child."

§

"I forgot how digging under a house kin be," Marcus said as he wiped his brow. "It wouldn't be hard work, but for them angles. I found myself in some peculiar positions, boss, but my side of the house is all done now, an' I got the footing for them jacks tamped down good."

"I'm jus' about done here, too," Willie replied, shaking the dirt from his hands. "An' James beat us both. He had the short sides of the house, but he got 'em both done. Don't know where he's gotten to, but I expect he'll be back."

"He hauling some of them wood blocks over to my side for the cribs. I told him to have himself a break, but he wouldn't hear of it."

Willie chuckled. It was only last summer that James had been calling for breaks practically every hour. Back then, his body wasn't used to the heavy work of construction, but now he had both the energy of youth and the stamina of a veteran builder.

Willie slapped the earth from his overalls as he stood up. "Best get on to the next thing, then," he said as he stretched his neck. "No use in wastin' time. We got to keep up with James, I reckon." He chuckled again.

"This foundation sure do need our help," Marcus said as he pointed to a peeling, cracked section. "Water damage, I expect. Being at the bottom of this hill and all."

"The fixing will be the easy part, save for it being so low to the ground. That's jus' simple reinforced brickwork.

The hard part is getting this house up, nice an' easy. Keeping it level so we ain't cause no structural damage."

"True," answered Marcus. "But don't worry none, I done this a half-dozen times, at least. Seem like anytime the Alabama floods, someone finds himself in need of foundation work."

"I knew I could count on you, Marcus." Willie clapped his foreman on the arm gratefully. "Let's get this thing done, an' I'll buy you your supper at Rosa Mae's."

The three men spent the rest of the morning preparing the house for lifting. They carefully inspected the joists again, positioned the I-beams, double and triple checked measurements, tamped down each of the remaining footings, positioned the jacks precisely, and carefully stacked a pile wooden blocks beside each jack to use for incremental reinforcement. Willie worked as carefully as always, with Marcus giving him advice along the way.

To rebuild the foundation, the house needed to be lifted a good two feet. The men jacked up the house slowly, one side at a time, in two-inch increments. The building creaked and moaned as each jack did its work, but that was to be expected. Getting the house to the two-foot mark, and making sure it was perfectly level all around, took an entire hour itself.

"We clear!" Willie finally called out. "We have her where we need her." He looked at his work as he walked around into the backyard. The fully built house looked as if it were hanging in midair. An eerie sight.

"Boss-man, the bricks is here!" Marcus called out as Willie heard a truck begin backing into the driveway. He motioned for James to follow him, then hurried to the driveway.

"One thing about Lovejoy's is they always on time," Marcus said as the truck came to a stop.

"True. An' they want their money on time too," Willie added. "Henry Lovejoy is good helping out in a pinch—these bricks is from his own back-stock—but he makes no bones about credit. That's why I purchased these up front. No back-billing to deal with."

"That was smart," said James. "I remember this one time, Cayson's regular supplier was out, an' we was in a real fix. David got so desperate he called on Lovejoy. Accounting thought they could wait till the build got underway 'fore paying. Don't you know, Henry Lovejoy himself came to the site, had his men take back every single brick. When he drove off, he yelled, 'Negro-owned business is business just the same!' I thought David was jus' about gon' hit the roof."

"Serves 'em right." Marcus said. "I bet that's the last time Cayson Construction ever begged a favor from Henry Lovejoy."

The three laughed heartily as the two delivery men began unloading the bricks. They were kind enough to roll each pallet-laden jigger as close to the house as possible, saving the three men the backbreaking labor of hauling.

"James, Marcus, go on an' get that next pallet prepared for unloading, help these good men out a measure. I'm gon' have me a look under the house, make sure none of them secondary beams is sagging."

"Boss, a house ain't meant to be up in the air like that. Secondary beams always sag some."

"I expect so, but it won't hardly take a minute to sister them up, an' we got us a few extra jacks anyway. Safety first."

"I can't argue there," Marcus answered as he slapped some dust from his pants. "You always so careful on our sites. An' let me tell you, the crew and I, we sure do appreciate it."

Willie smiled in response before turning to his cousin. "James, go ahead an' sign my name to the invoice when you done," he instructed. "Remember, it's 'Willie' with an 'ie' at the end," he teased.

"Aw, go on!" cried James with a laugh. "I can spell better than most. I won me some ribbons for it an' everythin'!"

Willie winked, then punched his cousin on the arm playfully before he strode back over to the house and disappeared around the back.

"I really did win me some spelling ribbons," James said to Marcus, who was visibly holding back a laugh. "An' in sixth grade, I even won the county bee."

Marcus finally burst. A great, long laugh erupted from his belly as James looked at him in consternation. "You something else, kid, you know that?" he finally managed, catching his breath. "Now can you explain to me how spelling gon' help us with these bricks?"

"I reckon it ain't," James admitted as they climbed onto the flatbed to start loading the pallet. "But it's still a fine skill to—"

—*Crash!*—

"What the hell was that?!" Marcus cried, looking up in alarm.

"Oh, Lord, the house jus' shifted! 'Round the far side there!" James cried, jumping down from the flatbed and running toward the house all at once. "Willie! Willie!"

Both men froze as they rounded the house. The horror saw didn't seem possible. The porch, running the whole side of the house, was now caved in. The I-beam lay knocked on its side, rolled over by the force of the porch. Two of the three supporting jacks were buckled, as if they were never capable of holding any weight at all.

Marcus fell to his knees, peering into what was left of the crawlspace. "Boss-man! Boss-man! Call out! Where you at?"

Silence.

"Cousin, this ain't no time for playing," James yelled from a place deeper than his gut. "How bad you hurt?"

Silence.

James got down on all fours, crouching as low as he could. He called his cousin's name again and again, but no reply came, not even a moan of pain.

"Stop!" Marcus cried, yanking hard on James' ankle just as he began to crawl into what little space was left. "You can't. Move even one little thing an' you could get yourself trapped too! The whole house could go. We got to go in from the front, where that jack's still holding."

"That's my cousin in there!" James shouted.

"An' that's the best boss I ever had! We'll get to him, but we got to be smart about it. Or else you gon' get yourself hurt, too."

One of Lovejoy's men appeared, a clipboard in his hand and terror on his face. "If I thought it was like this…"

he began, "I wouldn't have unloaded that last pallet. Damn those bricks!"

"Run for help!" Marcus commanded. There's a pay-telephone just on the corner."

"Surely!" The man dropped his clipboard and sped across the grass, running faster than he even knew he could run. As he flew, he called for his partner to bring the first-aid kit from the truck.

"I think I can see… I think that's his boot there." The tears in James' eyes hadn't started falling yet; they only welled and guarded his pupils. He hoped beyond hope—the kind of hope that was prayer itself—as he called for his cousin in babbling, incoherent words. He needed to hear Willie's voice, or to see him fighting to get free. He needed his cousin to move.

When there was no space left beneath James' eyelids, his tears began falling down his cheeks. "Willie," he choked out, "I need you. Brenda needs you. An' the baby! Willie!"

Sizing up the wreckage and doing his best to figure out a plan, Marcus said, "I'll go around an' see where we can start pulling wood from. Don't you move from here till I say."

"Jus' let me go in and get him." James swiped away his deluge of tears as he peered up from the crawlspace. "Please, Marcus!"

"No! You gon' get yourself hurt," he repeated, even more firmly this time. "You stay put, kid, you hear?"

"Then let's get to the other side of the house. Move!"

"James," Marcus began somberly, fighting back his own tears. "We gon' do all we can, I promise. But... you best prepare yourself. This don't look good."

Chapter 25

Interrupting her story, Stephen McLemore nearly ran Debra over with his words. "So, let me get this straight," he began sharply, tapping his expensive pen against a legal pad. "You're saying that Willie Taylor, who wasn't experienced in this type of work, was killed because a house with known foundation problems collapsed on him?"

Debra nodded. "That's one way to put it. But that's not all, there's more yet."

"One thing at a time! Did they ever do an investigation on this incident?"

"No, not really," she answered as she reached for her phone. "Big Jim strong-armed Willie's mama into signing away all her rights. He gave her a little hush money and swept the whole thing under the rug." She swiped a few times across her phone, then held up the screen for Stephen to see. "They never looked into the jacks, either, but a weekly in Lowndes County did run a story on Willie's death. Those jacks crumpled like paper lanterns—you can see it clear as day in the photo."

Stephen carefully considered the evidence before him. "That doesn't prove the jacks came from Cayson. Nor is it evidence of knowingly selling faulty jacks."

Debra smirked in satisfaction. "No, but the bill of sale, that *is* proof. With David's signature on it. And I know exactly where that document is. I can have it here tomorrow, along with something else you might want to see. The birth certificate of Ton—"

"—Well, Debra, what I'm about to say, I say to you as a friend, not as an attorney." He cut Debra off forcefully. "You can ahead with this thing and try to smear the Cayson name, but remember you'll also be smearing the name of the man you loved."

Debra looked up toward the ceiling in frustration. She refused to let herself cry; she pushed back the tears that were threatening to escape.

"You don't want to do that to him, do you? You said yourself that you loved David more than anything in this world."

"My love isn't in question. Our decades together isn't in question. My love was proven," she snapped.

"I understand that, but—"

"—It seems to me, Stephen, that if Cayson Construction really understood how faithful and loyal I am to David, they would make sure I was provided for." She paused as she bit back her rising emotion. "And McLemore & Tinsley wouldn't let that bitch Mary take everything. Not when she's not entitled to it."

"I'm sorry, Debra, I can't help you," Stephen said as he stood up from his chair. "You could petition the courts for part of David's estate on the grounds of your years together, but we couldn't represent you. And—as a friend—I have to tell you that without a single asset held jointly, your petition would likely fail. Mary and her children are the legal heirs to David's estate, including Big Jim's holdings. There's nothing I can do about that."

"Nothing you can do?" Debra bolted up from her chair. "Didn't you hear a word I just said?"

He ran his fingers through his thin hair, biding his time before he spoke and hoping this meeting would end before things got truly ugly. "Our hands are tied, I think you know that. I can't change the facts, and I can't change the law."

Debra's frustration turned white-hot. She began pacing the room to keep from screaming. "Were you not paying attention *at all*?! I just told you—"

"—Estates are passed through marriage, Debra. *Legal* marriage."

"Estates are also passed through blood," she hissed. "Or didn't you go to law school?"

"Insults won't change anything," Stephen growled. "And you know as well as I do that you're no kin to David. As his wife, though, Mary is."

"I'm not talking about Mary," Debra spun around, a vindictive grin crawling across her face. "I'm not even talking about David, now. If you'd let me finish, you might've realized that Mary's kids don't share the same bloodline as Big Jim." She threw her head back in satisfaction; she couldn't help but enjoy watching all three hundred pounds of Stephen squirm.

"You've gone from hearsay to nonsense!" Stephen's face crinkled in confusion. "What are you talking about now?"

Debra almost chuckled. "You've only been hearing what you want to hear! Think it through, Stephen. Big Jim has a granddaughter. She's his closest blood relative."

"Then you go ahead and find her," Stephen replied, viciousness in his voice. "It's easy enough to discredit so-called relatives. We do it all the time. Anyway, who knows where she could be now, or if she's even still alive."

"If McLemore & Tinsley won't help, I'm sure she will. Because I know exactly where she is—she's a good friend of mine." Debra narrowed her eyes. "Tonya Taylor-Walker. James Taylor's stepdaughter."

The blood drained from Stephen's face. "Stepdaughter?" he asked, his mouth gaping.

"You didn't manage to put that together, did you?" Debra chuckled. "Brenda married James after Willie died, but Tonya is *Willie's* daughter. You think you can follow all of that?" She took a second to let Stephen catch up as her eyes gleamed in triumph.

"David was the heir. You know that. I'm well familiar with Big Jim's will, it specifies 'To my son, David.'"

"But David was never adopted, *legally* adopted. He told me that a thousand times. And if this firm was worth even half your reputation, you would've already known all this!"

"McLemore & Tinsley don't make mistakes," Stephen pushed back. "And you've shown me nothing to prove the contrary."

"Just you think about it for a minute, Stephen. A grandchild is *hard* to miss. And a *black* grandchild? Do you think the public will believe you simply *forgot* her? When she's the *only* offspring of the son Big Jim killed... arguably for his success as a black man?

"That's a stretch, Debra, by any means." He'd intended the words to come out strong and firm, but the fear caused his voice to crack.

"It's not that much of a stretch, once the media gets wind of it. McLemore & Tinsley is a premier firm—for now.

But just how deep do you want to dig that hole for yourself, Stephen?"

§

"Dennis, do you have a minute? I need to talk to you about the Cayson estates," Stephen said as he stood in the doorway of his partner's office. It was late in the day and most of the office was empty, which is exactly how he wanted it.

"Yes, I heard that Debra stopped by. Unfortunate," Dennis replied. "You best tell me what she wanted, although I can guess for myself: she's still upset about David's will—or lack thereof, as the case is."

"Yes, she's still upset," Stephen began twirling a pen in his fingers nervously. "Not that I blame her, if I'm being honest."

Dennis shrugged. "There's nothing that we can do about her feelings. We deal with the law here."

"I know that." Stephen shook his head. "But Debra made some statements that… we may need to investigate."

A hearty laugh rolled out from Dennis. "Scorned lovers always have something to say."

"I don't doubt it, but I think there's a legitimate problem here. Maybe several problems, in fact." Debra's words—all of them—replayed in Stephen's mind.

Dennis didn't reply, but his raised eyebrows told Stephen to explain further. "There's a lot we need to cover, but the main thing, in terms of our liability, is… Well, it seems we may have missed something in our in due diligence. Big Jim may have had issue after all."

"That's not possible. We've worked with the Caysons for decades. We know that family inside and out."

"According to Debra, a man by the name of Willie Taylor was Big Jim's illegitimate son. He sired a baby named

Tonya before he was killed. Killed in an accident that could implicate Big Jim *and* David, no less."

Dennis sighed heavily. "Stephen, I'm getting too old for this. You'd better sit down and start from the beginning."

Unsure of where to start, Stephen took a seat and folded his hands across his large stomach. He explained as best he could. He'd had most of the afternoon to take in Debra's story, but he still couldn't quite believe it himself.

"That's one hell of a tale, Stephen," Dennis remarked when Stephen finally fell silent. "How much of that is true?"

"Enough of it to cause problems, especially since the granddaughter is alive and well and here in Montgomery. We never had cause to look into the Taylor family—we missed her completely. That really doesn't look good for the firm, especially with a racial component in play."

"And why didn't this Tonya come forward after Big Jim died? When a wealthy man passes, relatives usually come crawling out of the woodwork."

"I couldn't say. Debra and I didn't get that far." He lowered his voice and added, "And I didn't think to ask."

"Whatever the case, what does it matter now?" asked Dennis. "Big Jim is dead and gone. No court is going to exhume the body for a DNA test. Not on the *rumor* of a bastard child's child."

"The birth records are easy enough to trace, and the court already has a DNA sample. Remember that case, a few years back? When that so-called half-brother of Big Jim's tried to lay claim to the land in Mobile?"

Dennis blinked several times before speaking. "There is that," he admitted. "That could be something." He paused, biting on his lip. "As for the rest of it, it's ludicrous. There's no cause to implicate Cayson Construction in Willie's death. You said Debra had what?—one invoice and one newspaper clipping?"

"It doesn't really matter if she can prove it. News moves like lightening these days. Any race-scandal—half true, all true, or even an outright lie—will damage this firm. A full-twenty five percent of our clients are minorities, and almost all of them are African American."

Rubbing his temple, Dennis stood up and started pacing. Stephen knew this was a sign that his partner could see the storm ahead brewing. In fact, he suspected that Dennis could see it even more clearly than he could.

"Dennis, you want to retire as much as I do. Jess is primed to take over next year, and you have Howard finishing up his JD now. So I guess the question is: What kind of business do we want to leave to our kids? A respected firm with years of excellence, or one that's stained with the kind of blot that doesn't wash out?"

Dennis signed heavily again before he leaned back slowly in the chair. He took another deep breath and let his head fall back. His partner was right; if they handled this wrong, they'd be gambling their kids' futures too.

"If that's the case, we'd better jump on this quick, Stephen. Even if it means losing the Cayson account, we'll have to extend our full resources to Debra. Pro bono. Starting tomorrow."

Chapter 26

Tri-River Supermarket had the worst selection of mangoes Brenda had seen in a long time. She picked up each fruit, felt its over-softness, then tossed it aside. All she wanted for her birthday was one perfect mango: she didn't think that was too much to ask.

Her cell phone rang just as she gave up and sucked her teeth in frustration. "Mama," came Tonya's shaky voice. "Mama, are you and Daddy gon' be home tonight?"

"What's wrong, honey?" Brenda asked, alarmed. She'd expected the first words out of her daughter's mouth to be a bright, "Happy birthday," but Tonya's tone told Brenda that her daughter wasn't thinking celebratory thoughts.

"You and Mark have a dust-up?" Brenda continued as she walked slowly down the aisle. "You want me to make up your old room?" Tonya's marriage was generally smooth and happy, but every few years she and Mark had a wallop of a fight, and Tonya would retreat back to her girlhood home for a night or two. It was their way letting the worst of the storm die down, of waiting until they were ready to face the issue together.

"Naw, Mama, it's nothing like that," Tonya replied. "Nothing's wrong like that, and the kids are fine, too. But I do need to talk to you and Daddy. It's... *pressing*, I guess you'd say."

A thousand thoughts flew into Brenda's mind at once, but she forced her voice to remain calm and supportive. "Of course you can come by. Whenever you need to, baby, you know that. Now, why don't you tell me what's wrong?" She shooed away the produce attendant as he approached. Where had he been when she was looking for a perfect mango?

"Debra took me out to lunch today after we were done with our meeting at the community center. First Saturday of every month, remember."

"Debra? I'm surprised she showed up. She's in all sorts of rage these days."

"She's hurting, Mama. Confused. Angry too. She has every right to be."

"Maybe she does, but she shouldn't be pushing all that ugly on you." Brenda sucked her teeth again.

"She didn't push anything on me, we just had lunch. But she did have… things to say. Things that could affect our family. Maybe for the better."

"You know my feelings on Debra," Brenda scoffed. "I'd think twice about anything she tells you 'is for the better.'"

"But Mama, that's exactly what I'm doing—thinking twice. That's why I want to talk it all over with you. Trouble is, what I have to say, I don't think Daddy will take it well. Cook one of his favorites for dinner and Mark and I will come by after, okay?"

"Your Daddy's the one doing the cooking tonight, but I'll—"

"—Oh, no! I'm all turned around! I didn't forget, Mama, honest I didn't. Happy birthday!"

"Thank you, baby. But don't you worry yourself. You know I don't make a much of a fuss about my birthday anymore."

"Maybe we should do this tomorrow, then. I'm covering the early shift for one of my nurses, but I should be done by three o'clock."

"No, baby, come this evening. It's okay. Any birthday with family is a birthday to celebrate, no matter the circumstance. I'll look forward to seeing you this evening."

§

"I'll clear up the plates, then get the dishwasher loaded," Mark said as he rose from the table and collected

Brenda's dish. "The birthday girl shouldn't have to lift a finger tonight."

Brenda laughed. No one has called me a "girl" in years. The numbers on my birthday cake proved why.

"Thank you kindly, son," said James. "It sure was nice of you to bring us dessert. Caramel cake is my favorite."

"Geez, Daddy everyone loves caramel cake," answered Tonya. "It didn't take hardly any time to put together, either. It's the frosting that's the tricky part. Mark helped with that."

"I sure did, just like my grandma taught me. I still can't get it exactly like hers, though."

"I'll help you with the dishes," James said as he gathered up his own setting. "We'll let our ladies talk a spell."

Tonya shot her husband a look, reminding him that she wanted some alone time with her parents. Mark understood. "No, sir," he replied, "it won't take but a moment. Happy to do it. Rest yourself easy."

Tonya waited until her husband disappeared behind the swinging kitchen door. She'd worked out in her mind exactly the right words to say, and exactly the right amount of details to share with her parents.

"Mama," she began, "tell me the story of how you an' Daddy came together again."

Brenda had been waiting all evening for her daughter to broach the subject of Debra. Her wedding story was the last thing she expected Tonya to bring up, but she followed her daughter's lead.

"You know the story, baby. After I had you, your Daddy was helping me finish this house. I was living with my parents, but I saw him on most days—and on days when I didn't see him, he'd come asking after you, being your godfather and all. You took to him like he was your own father."

"Yep, you sure did, honey," James smiled widely, his heart full of pride. "Sometimes your mama would drive you over to my job site, just to get you to settle. I'd sit with you in the backseat—you wouldn't fall asleep unless it was in my arms. The other men on the crew mocked me something awful sometimes, but I didn't mind."

"And you'd think all that hammering and banging would *keep* you up," Brenda added. "But nope. So long as you Daddy had you, you'd drift right off."

James reached over and grabbed Brenda's hand, squeezing it tenderly. "An' from there, I guess what happened between us just came natural. I mean, I'd known your mama for a while by then—she jus' about knocked my socks off the first time I saw her—but it took a while before the Lord smiled on us. From there, we sort of grew *into* each other."

"And we were married two years and two days after you were born." Brenda smiled. "We picked the date special, in honor of you."

Tonya sighed contentedly, reveling in her parents' happiness. She hated to intrude on that bond, but what she had to say what needed to be said. Even if it pricked at old wounds.

"But that's not all of it, Mama, Daddy. Tell me the part that came before. About my father."

James nearly snapped from hurt in reply. "I *am* your father... Always have been."

Tonya scooted over in her chair, then rested her head on his shoulder. "Of course you're my father," she soothed. "Always will be. *My* Daddy. Nothing is ever gon' change in that respect. I never want to hurt you, no matter what. I need you to remember that." She took his hand in hers. "But biologically... we're cousins, once removed. My *biological* father was your first cousin."

James tried to smile in response, but he couldn't quite manage it. The pain of losing Willie surged with a freshness that not even decades of distance could erase. "Yes, my cousin and my friend. My mentor, too. On the day he died, I promised I'd always do right by you. And I have."

"Yes, Daddy, you have. One-hundred percent, and then some," Tonya assured him, her head still on his shoulder. "Every single day of my life."

"We've always been open with you about all that, there's no secrets between us," Brenda interjected. "We never wanted darkness clouding our family's light. But why are you asking about Willie now? When it was so long ago?"

"That's the thing, Mama, that's what Debra wanted to speak to me about today."

"Just like Debra to go poking sores that never quite healed up," she snickered. "What good could it possibly do to upset your Daddy like that? Or me? Willie was my first love, baby. You know I love your Daddy with everything I got, but there's no love like a first love." Brenda's eyes misted over just a touch.

"I'm sorry, Daddy, Mama, I really am. But I'm asking because I might be able to help Debra, an' you always taught me to help when I can, even if it's hard."

James looked at his daughter tenderly; deep pain still reflected in his eyes, but forgiveness for his baby-girl was there too. "That's exactly right. We do for others as best we can. But I jus' don't understand what my poor cousin has to do with Debra."

"Well, Debra spoke to counsel, and they believe I have a legitimate claim to part of Big Jim's estate. And I never once did think of it, but I am his blood—even if the man never so much as smiled at me. He's not my family in my eyes, but the law says different."

Her parents listened intently as Tonya explained the details, but the frown lines in around Brenda's lips screamed the skepticism that her mouth did not.

"All Debra wants is the house and the retirement account," Tonya finally finished, "but Mary's still not budging. Debra isn't near as greedy as you think, Mama, she just wants the basics, lifeline stuff."

"I'm not too sure of that."

"Mama, you don't give her enough credit. You two clash a bit—always have. But think about it. If Debra wanted David's money so bad, then why wasn't *anything* in her name? That's not how a gold-digger operates—it wouldn't make any sense."

James laughed before he could help it. "I do believe our daughter has a point there, Brenda my dear. Smart as a whip—you have to give credit on that one."

Brenda's nose crinkled in consternation. "I'll give her that much tomorrow. When my birthday's over," she admitted. She slumped in her chair, pouting just a bit, as her husband held back another chuckle.

"Now Mama, if I can be the one to keep Debra from poverty, I should. If I don't, I'm putting an old woman out on the street myself. An old woman who's been our friend most of my life. The woman who put me through college when we were going through that rough patch."

"She did do that," James agreed. "An' I never once had a scuttle with Debra myself. She's always been decent people, to my mind. If not, I don't believe David could've stayed with her—not after living through all those years of ugly with Mary."

"It's still an awful lot to ask of you," Brenda countered. "Friends are one thing, but it's not like she's family."

James patted his wife's hand, which told her he was deep in thought. Letting him ruminate, she took a long breath and held in her next words with no small amount of effort. James stroked his chin slowly as he considered all their daughter had just told them.

"I don't like it, personally," he finally began, "because you're *our* daughter, paternity be damned. But do I concede it would be the right thing to do. The woman has nothing now that's David's gone. Though I do fret on the strain this will put on you, honey. Depositions, lawyers… none of that gon' be easy on you."

"Daddy, I know court battles are hard. McLemore & Tinsley will take care of most of it, I expect, and the rest I'll figure out. Plus, the kids will be back at college in a month— none of this should affect them at all."

"Well, I don't like it," Brenda pronounced. "Wealth poisons, it doesn't heal. Our family may not be rich, but we've never wanted for anything. Willie provided me with a good start, even if he died before we were married. This house itself, for one thing." She gestured sweepingly around the dining room. "And you see this dining set? This is Willie's work. Our end tables, our bedroom set, our mantle—

all Willie's. Pieces he made on the side when he was building this house."

Tonya's look softened. "Mama, you never told me all that. How was I supposed to—"

"—An' Debra's mess is her own to clean up," Brenda continued. "You expect me to believe she's so scatterbrained that she never discussed this stuff with her *dying* husband? Is she so white she thinks money simply *exists*, like the air she breathes? That it doesn't come from hard work?" She crossed her arms in frustration. She hadn't earned much from her years as a music teacher, but combined with her James' wages and careful saving at Mark's direction, they'd grown their nest egg bit by bit.

"Mama, that's not exactly fair. I'll grant you some, but Debra does a lot of volunteering. And not just sitting on committees, either. She does the hands-on stuff, like we do. That's work, even if it isn't paid."

"Enough!" declared James. "Let's think this through proper. Based on what is, not what should and ifs." He leaned his head back. "Debra made her mess, true enough. But we're Christians, we forgive. An' money don't necessarily mean evil, let's not forget that. Not if we hold onto what's in our hearts first and foremost."

"Yes, Daddy, that's what I'm thinking. I prayed on it all afternoon. Money can do a lot of good, too."

Brenda looked at her husband with a gleam in her eye that evinced both aggravation and respect. "My husband the peacemaker," she muttered, more to herself than anyone else.

James stood up and called into the kitchen. "Mark, quite hiding, son. Come on in here. You're part of this family too, and I do believe we're in need of your calculating skills."

Chapter 27

"Because there's so much you don't know!" cried Tonya, finally cracking under the stress. "There's *reasons* why I can't drop the suit. Good reasons!" She punched her pillow before burying her face in it, crying.

She thought she'd been prepared for a court battle, but with the weeks now stretching into months, Tonya was exhausted, frazzled, angry, and terrified. Mary was challenging her claim at every turn, for no other reason than to spite Debra. McLemore & Tinsley had advised Tonya to bring suit for one-fourth of the estate; a huge amount financially, but only a few drops in the bucket when compared to Big Jim's overall holdings. Yet Mary was clenching every penny with an iron fist.

The strain was worse than she could've imagined. Tonya couldn't sleep through the night, and she was losing weight too quickly. Everything she said was analyzed, picked apart, and turned right back around on her by Mary's new lawyers. She'd given the same deposition at least three times, she'd been in court more times than she could count, and McLemore & Tinsley had submitted not less than six DNA tests on her behalf. With every challenge and every bit of legal gymnastics, Tonya's faith in herself waivered just a little bit more. Even though she was telling the God-honest truth, she felt like a liar, as if facts could dance around and reorder themselves when she wasn't looking.

"They turn everything around when I speak! They keep asking why I didn't bring suit sooner, like I'm guilty of something! And now I have to give *another* deposition tomorrow!" Tonya sobbed. "I don't even care about the stupid money! I never did!" She wiped her eyes and tried to steady her breath. "I'd quit this whole thing if I could!"

"You can quit anytime, baby," Mark said. "You know I'll support you." He sat down on the bed and guided her head into his lap as he forced a chuckle. "After all, what's a few million dollars between husband and wife?" She appreciated her his attempt at humor, but she had no laughter in her heart now.

"And I've missed so much work," she continued in frustration. "My patients. How can I care for my patients like this? And my staff... they count on me too!"

"I hear you on that, but let's talk about work later. Right now, I think we need to focus on bringing an end to all this."

"But I can't end it. I *can't*. If I do that, they might find out..." she choked back tears once again.

"You've done your best by Debra, you've done what's right. She can't expect you to go on like this forever. She asked a lot to begin with, and now look what it's doing to you."

She reached over to her nightstand and picked up the framed picture of her parents. "If this was just for Debra, I would've quit weeks ago, Mark. Even with her house on the line, I would've walked away. No, this is for Daddy… and Mama, too, I guess. But mostly for Daddy."

Confusion covered Mark's face. "Honey, your parents are okay. Even without any help from us, they've got enough to keep them going. For many years yet. I've managed their assets carefully."

"I know you have, but it's not that," Tonya replied. "Money is the least of it." She sat up, ran her hand over the damp patch of tears on her husband's knee. "It's… I mean, there's just so much you don't know. I've prayed and I've prayed, but I can't find a way out."

Mark's look turned grave, almost cold, as he asked, "What are you holding back? Tonya, we *don't* keep secrets from each other. We vowed that twenty-six years ago." He took a deep breath to calm himself. His eyes softened along with his voice. "Whatever it is, we can work it out together."

She rolled onto her back, staring up at the ceiling and trying to bring her words together in her mind. She couldn't face her husband as she spoke. "It's my deal with Debra. I'll give her her money, but that's not what I'm in this for."

"Baby, you're not talking sense. Come on, let's go through this step-by-step. Now tell me—"

"—I'm in it for Daddy. Because he's an old man now, and some wounds cut too deep."

"What wounds? Debra has nothing to do with your father."

"*She* doesn't, but David *did*. And if Daddy ever finds out… Oh, Mark! Daddy will be broken for the rest of his days. I don't see him ever coming back from it. He doesn't deserve that!"

She turned her head toward the window, away from Mark, and hugged the framed picture of her parents to her chest. "A lifetime of friendship, all a lie," she muttered. She suddenly shot upright, fear and anger and love propelling her. "Could you take a blow like that?! If you'd spent your whole life finding the best in people?"

"Baby, best you start at the beginning, because I'm still not following. What did David do?"

Tonya explained, beginning with Willie's death. The jacks. The signed invoice. The newspaper clippings. The hush money to Willie's mama Rita, recorded as a "miscellaneous" payment on Cayson's books. The pile of evidence Debra had shown her, evidence that all pointed to decades upon decades of lies.

Mark's face betrayed equal parts shock and concern. "Baby, you can't be sitting on a thing like that," he said firmly once his wife fell silent. "That's too much for anyone to hold onto on their own. And... I hate to say it, but I know you're right. That could *destroy* your daddy through and through. He's such a gentle soul."

Tonya again exploded into frustrated tears. "I know... I know! I should've told you, before, but I... thought..."

Mark's nostrils flared as he tried to put the pieces together. "So Debra knew about this for all these years?"

"No, no. She's only known since Big Jim passed and David got real sick. She just didn't know what to do with it. Would you?"

Even still, sounds to me like your mama's been right all along. She's been extorting you since David passed?"

"Of course not! Debra's not holding anything over me—she'd never do that. This was *my* idea, mostly. Our deal is, when I win the settlement for her, she'll hand over every piece of that evidence."

"Tonya, it's a fine thing to protect your own, but that if that came out in court, it could look real bad. Mary's lawyers could spin it something awful."

"I know that!" Tonya hissed frantically. "And her damn lawyers are circling me buzzards now. They keep insinuating I'm hiding something. And they're right—I am! All sorts of things!"

"I wish you'd talked to me on this!" Mark cried. "No wonder this is tearing you up. You're keeping too much from too many people—including me!"

"Tell me you'd do anything less if it were your parents!" Tonya shot, defiance in her voice. "I made that deal so they could finish their days on this Earth in peace!"

Mark fell silent, clenching his jaw as he thought. He started pacing the bedroom, muttering to himself, trying to think clearly through his shock, frustration, and anger. He'd watched his wife suffer over the last months—now he understood better. But how much deeper was this mess?

A good two minutes later, he finally nodded in agreement. "For me and mine, I'd likely do the same, yes." He took a seat in the wingchair in the corner, purposely putting some distance between himself and his wife. "And you're a good daughter for protecting your Daddy. But that deal is a cross on top of burden. How much of it could they prove, if it came to that. Did you put anything in writing?

"Jesus, Mark, I'm not that dumb. Debra and I didn't draw up a damn contract! Not even Stephen and Dennis know."

"And what about your birth father's... *accident*? Do Stephen and Dennis know about that?"

The soft brown pools of Tonya's eyes filled with even more misery. "Yes. It's the reason they agreed to take my suit. That's the other part of this story." She did her best to explain all of Debra's dealings with McLemore & Tinsley. "Debra *did* threaten to leak it all to the media, but she had a plan for talking to Daddy beforehand. She wouldn't blindside our family; she's a Christian, too," Tonya finally finished.

"Oh God, Tonya." Mark hung his head and began rubbing his temples with his fingers. With that hanging over you, maybe you should be honest and have done with it, even if it breaks your Daddy's heart. I'll even be the one to tell him, if you want. I'll explain how hard you tried."

"You'll do no such thing! I owe this to him, Mark. I owe him peace! Daddy didn't have to marry my mama. An unwed woman with a baby! In the 1960s? With us being Methodists? Think of it! And he didn't *have* to adopt me, either, and he didn't *have* to claim me like he did, like his own. Do you think I don't carry all that with me *all* my waking days? You think I don't owe him *everything* I got in me?"

"Your Daddy is a good man, I'm not disputing that. But I need to know you've thought this through fully. There's still a possibility of some justice for your birth father—that's not entirely off the table with today's technology. Are you're *sure* you want that evidence gone?"

"I'm sure. What good would that do? Big Jim is dead, David is dead. All I want is for my parents to live out their days in peace. I still have some faith left, Mark—I truly do, even with all this stress. I wish it were over, but I still believe there's a way for everyone to get what they need. And for

Daddy, all I want is to let sleeping dogs lie."

Chapter 28

When she heard Mark's car coming up the driveway, Tonya rushed to the window. He was late tonight. How he walked on his way into the house would tell her everything she needed to know about her husband's state of mind.

She'd called him earlier in the day and filled him in on the deposition. Stephen and Dennis had assured her that today had done nothing to alter her case—all it did was give opposing counsel the chance to file yet another motion. Another motion that McLemore & Tinsley would counter. Which would only lead to yet another deposition, and to yet another motion.

The case stretched before her, seemingly endless, but last night's cry had done her some good, as had the half-hour she'd spent in prayer in church first thing in the morning. She'd been calmer today than she had been in a week, and Mary's lawyers hadn't managed to rattle her—although not for lack of trying. Tonya loathed those men. Greasy, greedy, lawyers who gave the rest of the profession a bad name.

Mark's stride was cool but just a touch too fast, which meant something weighty was on his mind. As he approached the door, she darted back into the kitchen. Whatever he had to say, a plate of well-seasoned pork chops would help things along.

"Dinner's in ten minutes, baby!" she cried as Mark came through the front door. "Get yourself washed up and out of that suit."

Loosening his tie, Mark walked into the kitchen. "Thank you, honey, but we'd best put off dinner just yet. An idea's come to me, something we should discuss right away."

Tonya forced a bark of a laugh. "Since when can't we eat and talk all at once? Everything seems easier on a full stomach."

"That's just the thing," he replied as he walked over and pecked her on the forehead. "I don't think easy will do us any good just now. Full stomachs make for dull senses. What we need for the moment are sharp minds. Clarity of thought."

Tonya looked at her husband in bewilderment as worry crept through her. A husband who didn't want supper was a husband she hardly knew.

"Come on over here and set," Mark said, pulling out a chair. "Though I will say dinner smells mighty fine," he added with a hint of a smile on his face.

More confused than concerned, Tonya turned down the heat on the stovetop slowly. She thought about opening a bottle of wine but decided against it, then crossed the kitchen and took a seat.

"Now, I've thought this thing through," Mark began. "And I believe I have a way to speed things up a good pace, or maybe even put an end to it. Before the strain gets too much."

"You mean before something comes out that it shouldn't," Tonya muttered.

Mark sighed. "Well, yes, that too," he answered, squeezing her hand. "But not just that. We've got to get a measure of normal back around here. For both of us. And Thanksgiving is coming up quicker than you think. The kids will be home in a few weeks—we don't want them knowing about all this, at least not yet."

"I know, Mark. I had no idea it would drag like this. Almost three months now!"

Mark's face turned even more sober, although his eyes remained tender. "So my question to you is this: Do you really *not* care about the money? *Really* not care?"

Tonya's eyes narrowed. "I said as much, and I meant it. Avarice is a sin just as much as any other, and I'd trade every cent of that money and more for my family, you know that."

"Tonya, honey, tell me the truth now. There's no shame in it. Money is as much of a tool as anything else. So tell me, exactly *how much* don't you care?"

"I'll keep to what I promised Debra, that's the main thing." She looked down at her lap. "But as for us, I think I… it's not like I was hoping for…" She fell silent as the words twisted up her tongue.

"Because I work with other people's money for a living, baby. And I can tell you, after a certain point, more money doesn't mean more happiness."

"Yes, that's how I feel about it, too. Just look at Mary. She's got more money than God, *and* more coming her way, yet she's still a miserable old bitch. Always will be."

"Exactly. Your intentions are all good—I know that's the truth of it, Tonya—but we have to think clearly about a clear an exit strategy. So what do you *really* want from a grandfather who never once looked your way? Who's causing you all this misery even after he's dead?"

Tonya picked up a napkin and started twisting it in her hands, keeping her gaze trained on the papery fabric. "Well, I guess, I… I… wouldn't say no to *some*. Pay off the mortgage. See the kids through grad school. Maybe set aside enough to help them buy their first homes."

"That's my thought," Mark agreed. "And I'd add to that, some funds for our 401k. I'd like to add a measure of cushioning to our parents' savings, too."

Tonya swept up the remains of the napkin in her hands. "And something for a good cause, too. We can't just think of ourselves. Set up a trust for the community center, or establish a local scholarship. Something like that."

Mark grinned broadly. "I was banking on your saying that, baby. You're just like your daddy that way. I have something like that in mind, too."

Tonya smiled a smile despite herself as she nodded in reluctant agreement. "That's really all I'd want. We don't need millions and millions. If I wasn't hedged in on all sides, I'd take a settlement like that to put this all to rest. *If* I had the choice. A *real* choice."

"We're agreed then." Mark stood up and rubbed his hands together eagerly. "Now let's get to those pork chops before they dry themselves out. Because now I know exactly what to do."

§

"It's a bold strategy, I'll say that much," Stephen said as he considered Mark's proposal. "I don't know that it makes any difference legally speaking, but no judge would want to be seen as standing in the way of something like this. I'd expect he'd tell Mary to settle."

"Yes, especially with elections coming up next year," agreed Dennis. "But I also agree that this makes no difference in the legal sense. *How* you use your settlement is none of the court's concern, strictly speaking."

"I'm willing to put all this as a stipulation on the settlement," Tonya said. "Ironclad. I'd be under legal obligation. Most of the settlement will go straight into an escrow account."

"If that's the case, it's imperative that you understand: should you fail to meet those obligations, you'd likely face criminal charges," Dennis advised.

"I understand that. But the money won't even be in my name. Not really. McLemore & Tinsley can serve as executors, if you think that will help. I have no interest in touching those funds for personal use."

"That's easy enough to say now, Tonya, when this is all still speculative. But when the time comes, could you really part with so much money?" asked Stephen. "Because I'm not sure I could. An amount like that is life-changing."

"As long as Debra gets to keep her house as well, yes. This is what Mark and I want to do. There'll be plenty left over for us, anyhow."

"And we *do* want this suit to move forward," Mark added. "You said it yourself—this could go on for years!"

"This is our best chance at cutting Mary off at the knees and bringing this to an end," added Tonya. She slumped in her chair. "And honestly, I'm exhausted."

Mark reached into his briefcase and pulled out a folder of pie charts and graphs. "Look here, I've done the calculations. We'll slash our claim in half, to one-eighth of the estate. In round numbers, that's twenty-five million. We're willing to put seventy-five percent of those funds— almost nineteen million—right back into Montgomery. To enhance African American communities."

"It's an interesting strategy. Even if the judge didn't encourage her to settle, this would be hard for Mary to fight," Dennis remarked thoughtfully. "Again, legally, it makes no difference—she has the right to challenge until a court says otherwise, and even then she could appeal. But ethically... ethically she'd look like a poster child for the Jim Crow era. Would she really want that hanging over her family name?"

"If there's one thing Mary *does* care about almost as much as money, it's the Cayson name," Tonya agreed.

"It's a brilliant course of action, I'll grant you that. Financially, however, I can't advise you down this path," Stephen said firmly. "You'd have to sign a waiver absolving McLemore & Tinsley of fiscal mismanagement."

"Really, Stephen, *that's* what you're worried about? Mark and I will sign the damn thing. How much money does one family need, anyhow?"

"According to Mary Cayson, two hundred million dollars," quipped Dennis.

"Well, I'm not Mary Cayson. Debra isn't Mary Cayson. My family isn't Mary Cayson," Tonya said sharply. "There'll be more than enough left over for us."

"And you've talked to Debra about all this?" asked Stephen. "She might feel otherwise."

"She keeps her house, we'll fund her retirement account. Considering her situation—and the hell my wife has been though—that's more than fair," replied Mark, pushing the thought of Willie Taylor and the secrets Debra guarded from his mind.

"With this arrangement, everyone gets something they want, even Mary," Tonya continued. "Except for the house, she gives nothing to Debra—and certainly that's the best the old goat could hope for at this point."

The three men around her burst out laughing. Tonya couldn't help but join them.

As soon as Mark caught his breath, he picked up where his wife had left off. "We'll fund Debra beyond that," he said, pulling out another graph from his folder. "Our family will personally keep a minority percentage of the settlement, but nothing too extravagant in today's money. The lion's share will go into enhancing the city's underserved communities, which will only boost McLemore & Tinsley's public profile. Everyone wins."

Tonya shot her husband a look. A look of relief that spoke silent volumes: "And Daddy stays whole all of his days."

"If you're sure this is what you want to do, we'll get started this week," Stephen offered.

"I expect you to draw up the papers immediately," Tonya directed, her voice growing stern but not cold. "I'm trusting this firm to do what's right. Don't disappoint me. Be aggressive. I want Mary's signature by next week!"

Chapter 29

James called out, letting his daughter know that he'd let himself in with his key.

"Daddy, what are you doing here?!" Tonya cried from the top of the stairs. "I wasn't expecting you, and I sure am a mess." She pulled the kerchief from her head with one hand as she quickly patted down her hair with the other. "Hold on one second, I'll be right down." She ran into the bathroom, grabbed her laundry basket, then started down the stairs.

"I can carry that down for you, honey. No need to fuss."

"It's okay, Daddy, it's not heavy at all. I'm just trying to get things straightened up around here." She paused at the landing and kissed her father on the cheek. "You know I can't relax with a dirty house."

"You're just like your mama that way," James laughed. "She was up at six o'clock polishing and dusting. I can't say I detected anything resembling uncleanliness myself, but the piano sure does shine now. Heck of a way to spend a Saturday morning, though, if you ask me."

"Saturdays for cleaning, Sundays for services," Tonya recited as James put his arm around her for a quick hug. "She always told me that when I was little. Guess it stuck."

"Sure enough," he replied with a smile. "But there's plenty of Saturday left still. Let's you and me set for a minute, have ourselves a chat."

"Anything wrong? You usually call first."

James took a seat on the sofa. "Naw, jus' the opposite." He patted the cushion next to him, inviting his daughter to his side. "I did intend to call, but I was on my way back from Selma, an' before I knew it, I was here." He chuckled. "Sometimes driving goes quick like that."

"Selma? What were you doing all the way out there?"

"Well, perhaps I should've spoken to you on it first, but I got it into my head last night to go talk to Mary, so that's what I done today."

"Oh, Daddy... you, weren't supposed to step in. We're supposed to let the lawyers do all that."

"That may be, honey, but no lawyer in the world gon' substitute for familiarity. I've known Mary for a good bit more than half of my life at this point. That counts for something."

Tonya's face scrunched up as her emotions collided. She knew her father was right, but at the same time, she didn't like his taking on the extra stress—especially not when she was keeping so much from him.

James laughed gently. "You've made the same face since you were two. You can't keep your feelings bottled up, never could."

Not knowing what else to say, Tonya whispered, "It's complicated." At least that much was the truth.

"First, I have to tell you how proud I am of you. That settlement offer... it takes an awful lot of courage to do a thing like that. Walking away from more money than most of us would see in five lifetimes."

"I'm not walking away from it, Daddy. There'll be plenty left over for us, and the rest... I mean, who knows how many people it will help? If anything, Mark and I are walking *toward* the good that money can do. We haven't settled on how we'll use the funds yet, but we know it'll be for something that helps folks help themselves. Something that empowers our people."

James' heart swelled as he slipped one arm around his daughter and hugged her close. "Maybe your mama and I raised you right after all." He buried his face in her hair to hide the tear in his eye.

Tears formed in Tonya's eyes, too, but for a very different reason. Never in her adult life had she kept a secret from her father. It weighed on her heart, even if she was burying David's sins for her Daddy's own good. "So what exactly did Mary say?" she suddenly burst out, mostly to keep herself from saying something that she oughtn't.

"Well now, it seems her lawyers did say it's in her best interest to settle. Judge too. An' her sons want this over, so they can move on with their lives. But Mary, she's stuck on the house, like a mosquito on flypaper."

"Stuck on the house? I don't follow, Daddy."

"She's not gon' settle so long as she's got to sign the deed over to Debra. She's got that hate in her heart, an' she don't know how to let go."

"I don't know how you stand her, Daddy. That house means *nothing* to her, everything to Debra. I don't even think Mary's ever seen it from the inside."

"We all have faults, Tonya. Me an' you included. But there's always a way to make a way if we keep working at it. My cousin taught me that, and I see so much of Willie in you sometimes. He spent his life tryin' to make things better for the folks he loved, in his way." James clasped his hands together as he turned his heavy gaze downward. "And although Mary won't cooperate, I do believe there's a path *around* her bitterness. So honey… I know it ain't exactly fair, but I'm asking you to work jus' a little bit harder and make a way."

§

"Move out?!" cried Debra. "If I move out of this house, I'll never see the inside again! You know that as well as I do, James."

"Naw, it's jus' temporary. Three months, tops— probably less. For renovations."

"Three days or three months, it doesn't matter. If I leave this house, she'll find a way to *keep* me out."

"Debra," Tonya began gently, "the house won't be hers anymore. She'll have no right to force you out—even

Mary's won't risk to criminal charges just to spite you. At her age?"

"She should be in jail now," Debra growled under her breath. "For all the hell she's caused me."

"And you know how particular she is about her dress," Tonya continued. "Horizontal stripes? Think about it!"

James burst out laughing. Tonya joined him before she could stop herself. Mark got swept up in the wave. Within a few seconds, Debra was giggling, too. The sound rolled off the porch and echoed into the twilight of the backyard.

"We've been back and forth on this for three weeks now," Mark started as he caught his breath. "The old bat won't sign this house over to you, and she won't sign it over to Tonya, either. So what we need is a little creative accounting."

"Creative accounting doesn't sound like a way for me to keep my home, and renovations don't sound like a way to keep my memories. David and I made a life here. Chris and Lauren practically grew up here. This house is a lifetime."

"We understand, Debra. We're just coming at this thing from a different angle, although the goal of keeping you in this house stays the same." Mark continued, "We're betting that Mary will part with this *if* we stipulate that it's to be used for our foundation's office."

"We sure are fortunate this area is zoned for mixed-use," James added. "Office space under two thousand square feet is permitted. Lots of these homes have doctors or dentists on the first floor. This'll be much the same."

"Offices? Then where will I live?" Debra asked, truly perplexed.

"Right here," Tonya said brightly. "Or more accurately, about fifteen feet above right here."

Debra didn't respond. She looked at Tonya for a long moment, utterly puzzled and unsure of what to say.

"An' this way, you'll get to keep your home and your memories. Just at a higher elevation, is all." James' eyes sparkled mischievously.

"Y'all are having a laugh on me. What aren't you telling me? What am I missing?"

"Hopefully the same thing Mary will," answered Tonya. "She'll never suspect."

"Suspect what?! I can't fathom what you're talking about." Concern crept into Debra's eyes; she wasn't sure she was ready for what was coming.

Mark began explaining the plan. "Once the house is in the foundation's name—"

"—we jus' gon' lift the whole structure up an'—"

"—build a story underneath! For our office!" finished Tonya.

Shocked, Debra nearly turned green as the picture of the house that killed Willie popped into her head. "Can you do that?" she finally whispered." Can you do that… safely?" She ran her hand over her stomach as her insides reeled. "Safely… and without Cayson Construction involved?"

"Yep, sure can. An old buddy of mine will take care of all that. He has himself a shop specializing in this kind of work. After forty-five years at Cayson, I know how to keep this off their radar."

"Once that's done, our foundation will rent the top two floors back to you. For as long as you like. Fully paid for by the funds we're putting into your retirement account." Mark explained. "At market rate, too, so there's no impropriety. Like I said, creative accounting!"

James reached into his pocket and pulled out a well-folded piece of graph paper. "The way I figure it, we won't need to renovate your space at all, except for moving the entryway by a mite. Look for yourself."

Debra smoothed her hands over the paper as she studied the rough plans. Her parlor, kitchen, dining room, bedrooms—everything was there, all intact. Amazement filled her eyes as she met James' gaze. "I'd get to… keep everything? Just the way it is?"

"Except for that one change here," he began, pointing to his sketch, "it's gon' stay the same. We'll even keep this porch as-is, though I expect you'd want us to extend the stairs some. Fifteen feet is a mighty tall step."

Mark laughed. "That's a fine point, sir. Gravity judges us all equally. Safety first!"

With Willie and David shooting to the forefront of her thoughts, Debra looked Tonya knowingly in the eye. "You're going to save my home by jacking it up?" she asked as her eyes welled. "Tonya, honey, do you *know* what you've done?"

Chapter 30

"Mama, you look beautiful tonight! Spin around for me, let me see the back."

"Thank you, baby. Your Daddy bought me this dress special for tonight," Brenda replied as she twirled slowly around. "He came shopping with me and everything."

"Sure did. We spent a whole day going to jus' about every fancy store in town. Glad we did, too—I haven't had occasion to put on a new suit in more years than I care to say."

"Daddy, you look mighty fine, too," Tonya said as she smoothed his lapels back down. "Very handsome."

The pride in his eyes gleamed brightly as James spoke his next words, "Some things are still worth getting dressed up for, honey, and this… is sure one of them. Your mama and I, we're jus' so proud. Of what you've built here, and for what all this means to our family. Our *whole* family."

Her heart nearly burst when she saw her father's glistening eyes; never once in her life had Tonya seen him misty-eyed. She reached her arm around him for a hug, then pulled her mama into the embrace, too. The trio stayed huddled together for a long, long, moment, all pretending to hide their tears from each other.

"Tonya, can I have a word with you for a minute?" Debra asked as she approached. "I hate to steal you away from your parents, but..."

"She's all yours," Brenda said brightly, quickly composing herself. "We know our daughter is awfully busy these days!"

The past few months of Tonya's life had been a flurry of activity. Once Mary had agreed to settle, Tonya became so busy that she had to take a leave of absence from the hospital. She hated leaving her ward, but every day she reminded herself that she was doing good. A thousand things needed to be taken care of before the foundation could launch—the office needed building, equipment and supplies for the staff needed purchasing, board members needed soliciting, and Tonya had just about worked herself into exhaustion recruiting a talented director to run it all. Mark had deftly handled all the finances and other paperwork, while Tonya focused her efforts on the more hands-on aspects. James had volunteered to work on the renovations during the building phase.

With the office complete and the basics in place, in the last three months, Tonya had built a coalition of minority business owners, all committed to supporting African American homeownership. Brenda had been by her daughter's side the whole time, volunteering as an administrative assistant. Any business who joined the coalition received a grant from the foundation to underwrite their incentives. Whether it was a couple buying their first house, or a family home in need of repairs, the foundation culled every available resource in Greater Montgomery under one roof. Tonight, financial planners and realtors mingled with carpenters and plumbers—all dressed in their best for the opening.

"If I didn't see it with my own eyes, I could hardly believe this," Debra began as she led Tonya away from the crowd. "And all of it happening right under my parlor."

Tonya laughed, a sweet, blissful sound. "That's right! We're a one-stop shop!" she agreed before her voice turned soft and somber. "But none of this would've been possible if you hadn't told me the truth about my birth father."

"That's exactly what I want to talk to you about," Debra replied. "It's been eating me up since the day David first told me. Maybe he was different as a young man, I don't know. But the man I knew, he never would've... he couldn't ever have..."

"I know. I understand. Not the David I knew, either. I can't reconcile it myself."

"But I want you to know, in his last months, he talked on it all the time. On his good days, and on the days when he could hardly string words together. He wanted to confess to your father, but he didn't have it in him. He had a terror of death—he needed to leave this world with his best friend by his side."

"I can't say I understand how he kept such a terrible secret all those years," Tonya said, fighting back tears, "but what's done is done, and I guess we all have regrets."

"For what it's worth, I don't think he could bring himself to hurt your father again, either. He just couldn't."

"Yes," Tonya agreed, "Daddy *shouldn't* know. That was the right thing to do, in an odd way. As much as it pains me, it's the right thing to do."

Debra grabbed Tonya's hand and squeezed it quickly. "I'll never tell. Not ever," she promised, her whole heart gleaming in her eyes. "There's been more than enough hurt to go around, and I love your Daddy, too."

"Thank you, I know you won't." Tonya dabbed at her eyes, trying not to smudge her mascara. "I will too—I'll take it to my grave, if it comes to it. I thought the guilt might undo me, but what we're doing here tonight… somehow the burden isn't so heavy now. Daddy built these walls himself, that makes it easier."

Debra reached over enveloped Tonya in her arms, holding her tightly. The embrace became both a bond and a vow.

As the long hug ended, Debra said, "Honey, I know I can never make things truly right, but I do want to… make amends, of a sort. On my husband's behalf—as well as my own."

"You gave me the records, that's all I wanted. Daddy will be safe and happy for the rest of his days, now. All those files are… gone, ashes. Dust to dust."

"I promised I'd give them to you, and I'm happy I did." Debra smiled sadly. "But that's not what I mean. Let me… give you my time."

"Your time?"

"Yes, I know I asked a lot of you. I pushed you into a corner, of sorts, and that's on me. I was desperate. When we started, I barely had a hope left, yet… you've made things right—for just about everyone."

"We work for what's right. Everything my parents have ever told me about my birth father—about Willie— points to that. So I guess I really am his daughter too."

"I never knew Willie, but I believe the best of him is in you. I think the best of *all* your parents are in you. And while I know I can never make up for everything, I would like to volunteer here at the foundation—in any way that I can, for as many hours a week the staff needs."

The smile that spread across Tonya's face was pure, joyful light. "We'd love to have you! You've done good works for years—your experience speaks for itself. Mark and I will find a place for you before we hand operations over to the board."

"It's the least I can do. You're building so much here, and I'll be honored to be a part of it." Debra paused before adding jokingly, "Plus, my commute will be a breeze!"

"Tonya!" called Mark from the head of the room. "Baby, it's nearly time! We need you!"

A stream of caterers appeared from the next room, carrying trays of champagne in fluted glasses. Each guest took their glass, readying themselves for the opening announcement.

Once the crowd had settled, Tonya took the microphone. "Good evening ladies and gentlemen," she began, ebullience in her voice. "Tonight, I'm pleased to welcome you to the Willie Taylor Foundation for Home Ownership."